Invincible

Books by Kay Brooks

The Row Series:

Spicer's Challenge

Dreams Fulfilled

Newfound Love

Persistent Intruder

Love Again

Shadows of Déjà vu

Victory Hill Trilogy:

Northwest to Love

Journey Back to Love

Possessed by Love

Biographies:

The Dancing Couple

I've Still Got Sand in my Shoes

Invincible

By Kay Brooks

Published by KDB Manuscripts, 2022

Front Cover Design by
SelfPubCovers.com/RLSather

Invincible

This is a work of fiction. Similarities to real people, places or events are entirely coincidental.

First edition, April 1, 2023
ISBN: 978-1-7354278-5-0

Published in the United States of America

To: Beth

Who is invincible herself

PROLOG

Couldn't have been a more perfect day, Savannah Hughes thought as she unlocked the door to her condo. Hard. Busy. Endless emails. But perfect, she conceded as she kicked off the five-inch spike heels, tossed her keys into the ceramic bowl on the narrow table next to the entry, reached to turn on the small lamp.

She was petite with a round face, creamy complexion, big brown eyes and turned up nose, long blonde hair that she preferred styled on top of her head for a more professional image. She pulled the pins out of her hair, tossed them into the bowl with the keys.

The hairs on her arms lifted a half-second before the fist plowed into her face and she fell unconscious to the floor.

Savannah awakened moments later, her chin resting on her chest. She blinked in confusion. What had just happened? Did she just black out?

She moaned as she shifted, moved her jaw left to right as she tried to raise a hand to her throbbing head only to discover her arms and legs were strapped tightly to a chair. Her eyes flew round when memories of the fist returned. Her head still lowered, she peeked side to side. It was dark except for the light from the lamp on the table near the front door, but she was certain she was still in her condo, held captive in one of her dining room chairs.

She jumped when a deep gravelly voice shouted. “Where is she?”

“Who?” Savannah jerked alert, stared at the stocky shadow, cried out when a broad palm slapped her face.

“Don’t play with me, bitch. You know who I’m talking about.” He gave her another fist punch. “Where is she?”

“Who?” She whimpered, the right side of her face stinging from the blow. “Who?” she repeated. “I don’t know who you’re talking about,” Savannah stuttered, her chin trembling as she righted her head. Tried to identify him but only detected shadows.

She gagged at the metallic aftertaste of blood in her mouth. “I don’t- “

She flinched at the flash of movement, bellowed at the hard blow to her left eye.

“Why are you doing this?” She screamed, blood splattering from her mouth. “I don’t know who you are talking about.”

“Don’t fuck with me, bitch,” he barked. “Hayley Turner. Where is she?”

Savannah breathed in sharply. She tried once again to focus on the shadow. Did she know him? Had she met him somewhere? Her left eye was almost swollen shut. Semi-darkness prevented recognition, but she heard the venom in his voice, felt the cruelty in his fists.

Sweat beaded her forehead as she realized she was in a very precarious situation with an evil and dangerous person.

Hayley had cautioned her to be careful. To always be alert to her surroundings. Warned her there might come a day her world would be turned upside down.

But things had been going so smoothly, peacefully, for two years Savannah was certain they might be in the clear.

Now, she feared history was about to repeat itself as images of another gruesome murder flashed through her throbbing head.

"I'm sorry. I can't help you. I've never heard of Hayley Turner," she whispered, resigned that her night might not end as planned.

Savannah let out a high-pitched blood-curdling scream when his wood baton struck her right knee. She was sure she heard the bone break. He punched the round end of the stick into her stomach, so hard, the chair fell backwards, and her head crashed against the oak hardwood floor.

She gulped when his big hand grabbed the front of her dress at her chest, pulled her up right, then slapped her again.

Despite the pain, anger against the bully engulfed her. She was furious and annoyed to be so helpless. Her shoulders tightened, jaws clenched in a fierce rage as adrenalin pumped through her body and she shook the chair uncontrollably side to side, the whitened knuckles of her hands clutching the arms of the chair, almost lifting the chair up and down.

She glared at the shadow with her good eye then flinched when he raised his hand.

"I DON'T KNOW," she shrieked before the blow.

"Why?" she sobbed seconds later in defeat, "Why are you doing this?" Her head snapped backwards every time he hit her until she lost consciousness.

Savannah awakened in a dark, confused fog. Pain engulfed her – in her face, her head, her legs. Everywhere. She inhaled the stench of his sweat, her urine as his fists caused her to lose control of her bladder. Heard his heavy breathing, felt nauseated from the metallic taste of blood that had pooled in her mouth, some of it drooling out the sides.

She experienced a skewed sense of time. How long had he been here? How long would he beat her? Would she even survive?

How did he even get into her apartment? Where was the building's security? She wondered. She was certain she had been screaming. Why hadn't her neighbors heard her? Come to check on her? Rescue her?

Her chin resting on her chest, her eyes darted left and right, she prayed for an escape.

She was certain if she raised her throbbing head, she would experience another blow. Her pounding heart roared in her ears as she tried to shift her arms and legs only to find they were strapped so tightly she was sure the ties were cutting into her swollen limbs.

"Please stop," she finally raised her head and whimpered, cringed from the raised hand.

One thousand miles away

"She unlocked the door, comma, tossed her keys into the ceramic bowl on the narrow table next to the door, period. Kicked off the five-inch spike heels, comma, let out a sigh of relief period. Next line. She reached to turn on the lamp, jumped when she heard a noise only to be greeted by a sharp fist in her face before falling unconscious to the floor, period."

Hayley Turner smiled as she dictated, setting up the beginning of her new murder mystery. The victim was a female, but Hayley imagined the face of William Ortiz, the man who had attacked her, almost killed her five years earlier.

She had recovered; her testimony and friend's backup documents put him in prison for the rest of his life.

Hayley killed Ortiz over and over as he was the face of all the victims in the six books she had written since that attack.

She leaned back in her chair, fingered the gold Celtic Knot Necklace that rested between her breasts. Sought the strength, courage and tenacity she needed from time to time.

Designed in Ireland, the three Trinity loops overlapped; the two outer edges lined with small diamonds – her birthstone – to shape a heart. A single carat diamond sparkled from the center. It had been a gift from her father during one of the lowest points in her life. She glanced at the note that had been attached to the gift – *Invincible like the diamond.* She'd framed it, set it to the right of her flat screen monitor where she could view it whenever she needed encouragement.

Hayley squared her shoulders, sat stiffly upright, and bared her teeth as she switched to the keyboard, typed the imagined blows that pummeled and killed her victim. Hitting the keys somehow gave her the satisfaction as if she'd delivered the blows herself.

You'd think the hate would have diminished by now, she thought briefly. But it never did. Each blow was as strong as when she experienced them herself.

It was a grisly murder, and the victim wouldn't be found for two days. Didn't deserve the end she got.

Chapter One

Hayley Turner sensed something was off as soon as she stepped outside the drug store. She felt the itch between her shoulder blades, sudden chill down her spine, quiver in her stomach. Someone was watching her.

Her hand subconsciously touched the Celtic Knot Necklace nestled between her breasts, beneath the white Regency shirt. Her worry stone during times of stress, duress, uncertainty.

She'd lived in the town for two years and had never experienced the prickle until now.

She turned in the direction of her car, her eyes darting left and right as she scanned the sidewalk ahead of her, searched for anything out of the ordinary.

Her heart skipped a beat when she glanced across the street, caught sight of the man seated at one of the tables outside the Main Street Café. Made no bones about the fact he was the new kid in town. Simply leaned back in his chair, ankle resting on a knee, arm on the table. Dark sunglasses covered his eyes, but she perceived his intense gaze loud and clear.

She swiveled to study the display in the *Blooms Galore* flower shop window but scrutinized the man's reflection in the glass as he rose, left money on the table, crossed the narrow Main Street toward her.

Coal black jeans covered long legs, a cinder gray crew neck sweater his arms. He hadn't changed, Hayley decided as she contemplated his loose athletic saunter.

What was Liam Walker doing in Champlain, Vermont she wondered.

Her nemesis, jailer, adversary, Liam was also her buffer, self-defense instructor, techie and bodyguard for almost five years. He'd been invisible the last two years, once he was assured safety parameters were in place and she could survive on her own. He might not have been nearby, but she always felt he was looking over her shoulder with everything she did.

Her heart lurched as Liam was also her only contact with her father whom she hadn't seen since the Ortiz trial. An only child, she'd lost her mother to a freak accident when she was sixteen, so her father was the only family she had. Was Liam here with bad news? She worried something might have happened to her father.

She didn't realize she'd held her breath until she exhaled at the sound of Liam's deep voice.

"We need to talk," he stated, his hands in his pockets as he casually studied the window display from the far end of the flower shop.

Hayley stiffened, acknowledged him with the slightest tilt of her head before stepping past him toward her car parked just down the block.

Liam Walker followed Hayley's burgundy Mazda in his black Dodge Ram truck. He was familiar with the directions to her mountain hideaway but gave her the space. *Lead, follow or get out of my way* had always been her motto. He was also aware that she wasn't a fan of taking orders; being second in command.

He'd driven all night, was grateful when his tracker zeroed in on her as soon as he hit the town limits. Wasn't sure which shop she was inside but once he spotted her car, he'd decided to stop. Appreciated that he'd had a chance to get a second wind, enjoy a cup of coffee while he waited for her to finish her errands.

He studied the rural terrain during the six-mile drive to her house nestled in the center of two-hundred acres of woods on the edge of the Green Mountains. Nothing much had changed since he was last here – thick woods, scattered houses, signs to beware of moose and bears. Same dairy farm with open fields, big barns and farmhouse in the distance.

He slowed when she turned onto the non-descript, almost hidden drive. Followed her around the curve and waited as she keyed in the code at the gated entry located further inside the woods. Hesitated to be certain the iron bars closed behind him before tailing her down the long drive.

He made a mental note that the dense woods would need another clearing in the coming weeks. Open spaces prevented dark hideaways and sudden ambush from dangerous intruders.

He smiled when they rounded the bend and saw the bright yellow mums and black-eyed Susan's interspersed in the beds across the front of the house. Purple and yellow pansies glowed in two pots on the front porch.

He recalled she'd taken a week in the spring after the release of her fifth book, to work on the landscaping – planted, mulched and tilled the barren earth. Was pleased she'd continued the transformation with the bright flowers of the season.

The house was suited for the three-quarter acre lot that offered enough open space for light but not be as visible overhead via helicopter or drone. Tall maple and oak trees surrounded the house that had been cleared of undergrowth, hiding spots for trespassers.

It was a two-story Tudor style – three bedrooms, two and half baths. Hayley had designed the house, her father had built it, he oversaw the construction. Installed the cameras – some she was unaware of – so he could keep her safe.

The narrow front of the house hid the extended depth of the interior. The roof line was split with a crossed gable roof over the garage, another over the second-floor bedroom. Light and dark gray fieldstone covered the bottom level of the house with lighter gray vertical siding around the windows and above the garage doors that were designed to look as if they opened outward but propelled upward instead.

Originally a one-car garage, Liam had expanded it to two to offer more open space, prevent anyone from sabotaging the car or ambushing her should they get inside. He pulled into the clear and vacant second bay. Waited for the doors to close behind them.

Hayley wasn't aware he intended to stay so he decided to leave his duffel bag in the truck.

He followed her into the house. Knelt to receive and pet seventy pounds of rich mahogany fur that greeted, almost toppled him with much excitement. Another concession to independent living for Hayley, Liam had trained Murdock, a Belgian Malinois security dog as a pup to guard Hayley.

"I was surprised you didn't have him with you in town."

Liam scrutinized Hayley as she deposited her reusable totes on the bar in the kitchen. It didn't surprise him that she hadn't spoken. He was sure her brain was frantically trying to determine why he was there.

"Savannah Hughes was murdered last night." Liam sat in one of the chairs at the oak clawfoot table in the dining area of the kitchen. Stretched his legs out, crossed his feet at his ankles, rubbed between Murdock's ears when the dog settled beside him, rested his head on Liam's lap.

"That's not possible," Hayley contradicted as she set a cup of cup of coffee, she was certain he would want in front of him. "I just got an email from her this morning. She talked about the release of the new book. How they had a celebration at her work yesterday afternoon."

"Check it," Liam's deep voice ordered as he stirred in the creamer.

He knew for a fact her friend was dead. He'd gotten a call from his source at the police station, viewed the bludgeoned body before they removed it from her apartment. It had not been pretty; he was glad Hayley would never have that memory to live with.

Like the memory she had of another friend.

"I read it this morning," Hayley corrected herself as she closed her laptop, nudged it aside on the bar. "She sent it late yesterday."

Hayley sighed heavily as she perched herself onto one of the bar stools. Her jaw clenched, she rested her elbows on the counter, her head between her hands.

"What happened?" She exhaled sharply as she stared at the black and gray speckled countertop.

"Someone apparently broke into her apartment, was waiting for her when she got home." He didn't want to describe the gruesome scene.

"What happened?" Hayley repeated, her sage green eyes bored into him as she looked up, challenged him to continue.

Liam cast her a veiled glance over the rim of the cup before taking another sip. Hayley was always one for detail; debated how much she would settle for. He set the cup down, leaned forward with his elbows on his knees.

"She was beaten." He paused a moment when he caught Hayley intake a sharp breath. Imagined she was remembering another beating. "One of her neighbors got home late, noted her door was ajar. Called to congratulate her on the book then went to check on her when she didn't answer her phone."

Hayley's mouth tightened into a straight line as she stared into Liam's whiskey brown eyes, was certain he was holding back. Thick dark brown hair was combed back from his broad forehead, the ends just brushing the collar of his sweater. The last time she saw him, Liam had a handlebar moustache, but he'd allowed it to fill out, so now a trim chin strap beard covered the lower portion of his face.

Liam sighed.

"I got a call, checked it out, then informed your father. He didn't want you to hear about it on the TV, so he sent me here to tell you."

"I need to go home," Hayley decided.

"You know you can't. They will be looking for you."

"They already are," Hayley snapped as she jumped off the stool, paced to the sliding door that led to the back deck. "Have been for over five years now." She wrapped her arms around her middle, stared at the line of trees along the edge of the woods. Studied the stack of pavers she had started collecting for her patio project.

Murdock sat beside her, leaned his mahogany body against her leg. She absently brushed her fingers behind his ear to reassure him she was okay before hugging herself once more.

Liam studied her. Appreciated the slim shoulders, narrow waist, long legs beneath the jeans. She was average height, but he knew the slenderness disguised her strength; the fierce powerhouse he had trained.

Dark auburn hair was pulled back into a braid that hung half-way down what he'd always thought was the most beautiful, graceful hourglass back he'd ever seen.

Hayley Turner had been his obsession both personally and professionally for five years now. He had protected her, trained her, travelled with her, oversaw the construction of her house and installation of security cameras when she finally conceded she needed surveillance safeguards.

She was the strongest woman he knew considering all she had been through.

It was his job to monitor her every move, report to her father on a weekly basis. He knew her routines, secrets, habits. Beheld her fitful sleep and cries in the night as she struggled with the fears and phobias she'd been forced to live with. Understood her sorrow and frustration.

He'd taught her self-defense, was confident she could defend herself but if his suspicions were correct, she would need backup. She was too isolated should she need help on the spur of the moment.

"She was probably killed because of me," Hayley murmured softly.

"Maybe. We don't know for sure. It could be a random B&E; we'll have to wait and see. Until then, your father wants you to be more careful. Wants me to stay with you until they've found who murdered her."

Liam anticipated her reaction. Watched her arms drop to her side, her hands shape into fists before she turned slowly to give him a glowering suspicious look.

"Not possible. This place isn't big enough for the two of us."

"I oversaw the construction of this house, you know better."

"Dimensions don't matter. You and I have never been able to be civil around each other for any amount of time. We'll kill each other."

Liam raised an eyebrow, nodded his head, studied her. "I'll be gentle."

"I won't."

"I'm following orders."

"I'll talk to my father."

Liam wasn't about to let on that it was his idea, not her father's, that he stay with her. He wasn't certain what to expect from this unexpected murder. His job was to protect her, and he had too much time invested in training and protecting her to do nothing.

He shook his head.

"It has already been decided."

"I've lived here for two years now. Nothing's happened."

"And now your friend has been murdered. We can't be sure what she told her killer. Whether he'd been hired by Ortiz."

"You don't understand," Hayley stepped toward him, threw her hands in the air. "Savannah didn't know anything. She was simply covering for me. She knew I needed a front and offered to be my buffer. She didn't *want* to know anything else. Not even where I live. We communicated by email; I sent my manuscripts to her electronically. She always said that way she didn't feel like she was lying if anyone asked."

Liam leaned back in his chair, ran a finger up and down the handle of the cup. "Doesn't matter. Until it is determined why she was murdered, I'm staying."

"Savannah was my friend. My *second* friend to die because of me."

"Judith Toliver's death was not your fault."

"That may be," Hayley paced back toward the door, "but she still died. And her murder was the beginning of my hell."

She turned to plead once more. Studied his set chin, piercing eyes as he returned her stare.

"Liam, you know we don't get along." She argued.

"You write all day we'll hardly see each other."

Liam mentally winced at the slip of tongue. Hayley wasn't aware of the security app on his phone that alerted him to every move she made.

"How do you know," Hayley wondered.

"Know what?" He stalled.

"That I write all day."

"Isn't that writers do?" Liam brushed it off.

"Not necessarily," she contradicted. "And I eat at odd times – sometimes I don't eat."

"So," he shrugged a shoulder, "there's plenty here for me to do."

Hayley crossed her arms across her breasts in frustration. "I'm not cooking for you."

"Didn't ask you to. I might not cook for you."

"I don't have time for anyone else in my life right now," she threw her hands up, paced between the bar and the back door.

"You won't know I'm here," he assured her.

That's impossible, Hayley thought as she turned to glare at him. Liam Walker was always on her radar.

"I need to have quiet when I write. No music. No blaring radios. No distractions."

"I've got my ear buds."

"I just can't concentrate when anyone else is around," she exclaimed in frustration.

"Get used to it," Liam stood, marched to the sink where he rinsed his cup, left it in the basin.

He moved toward her, wrapped his hands around her upper arms as he stared down at her.

"Hayley, we've been lucky not to have had any problems for two years. But we knew it couldn't last forever." Whiskey brown eyes probed her sage green eyes as he gave her body a slight shake of reassurance.

"This house is big enough for the two of us. Between the fitness room in the basement, clearing that needs to be done in the woods, hiking trail, there's plenty for me to do. Maybe I'll clear another trail."

He nudged her aside when he realized he'd had another slip of his tongue. She wasn't aware of the cameras in the woods.

"I'm going to take a short nap. In the spare bedroom. Don't bother me."

How did he know about my hiking trail, Hayley wondered as he headed up the stairs.

Hayley's head lolled side to side, her body flinching as she relived the nightmare that hadn't plagued her for months.

There were loud voices – Judith's screams of pain, the man's angry grunts and shouts – as his fists pounded her friend, demanded she tell him where she hid the evidence.

Her heart racing, Hayley took in a sharp breath, tried to back further into the wall as she viewed the man reach for the handgun. Saw the sudden flash, then the slow motion of the bullet as it struck Judy in the forehead, her head jerking backwards as she fell to the floor.

Hayley covered her mouth, tried to smother the scream when Judith's face turned toward her, the red hole above eyes that stared blankly at her.

Hayley moaned, twisted onto her side as if to run away. Aware the man would come after her next.

"Savannah," Hayley cried out when she looked back, found Savannah's face staring at her instead of Judith's. The red hole was gone but Savannah's eyes glared as if saying *you did this to me.*

Hayley's hand flew to her chest, clenched the necklace around her neck. Her finger feathered the diamonds that formed the outline of a heart, sought the lone gem in the center. Sought her link to sanity. Comfort. Peace.

She bolted upright in the bed. Gasped for breath as her heart raced, the beats pounding loudly in her head. Her face glistening with sweat, she felt Murdock's wet nose beneath her hand, heard his whine, realized the dog is trying to comfort her.

She threw back the covers, nudged the dog back to his bed. Moved to stare out the window at the shadows in the back yard. Ran her hands through her loose hair before wrapping her arms around her stomach, as she tried to control the nausea and breathlessness.

Damn the man, she fumed silently. She would not let William Ortiz dominate her life again she vowed.

Things had been going so smoothly. She had a promising modeling career, independent life sharing an apartment with her best friend. Until she came home one evening, witnessed Judith's murder, then was beaten herself and left for dead. After months in the hospital and rehab, she beat the odds. Regained her memory, healed her wounds and testified against Ortiz and his organized crime.

Then had to disappear when she and her father received death threats after his conviction.

It was bad enough she'd been forced to give up her dream, literally disappear off the face of the earth. But she'd refused to give in completely. She'd trained and escaped to Champlain, Vermont where she lived under an assumed name – Amelia Cox. Pursued her other passion, the written word. Now wrote murder mysteries as Jillian McLeod but was unable to publicly enjoy the benefits of her success. Savannah had done that.

She had success and she was safe, but it had had cost her. She hadn't seen her father since her court appearance. She had no real friends because friends meant questions, sharing secrets. Her only links to her former life were Savannah, her image in the publishing world, and Liam.

Now, Savannah had probably been killed because of her.

Hayley rested her forehead against the window and sighed. Once again, her life was in turmoil, being turned upside down.

Liam had trained her to be strong, resilient and invincible but she wasn't certain she was up for a second round.

Liam stared from the dark hall. Angry that Hayley must once again suffer with the nightmares in silence. By herself. With her mother deceased and her father living with his own death threats, there had been no one to be with her during her recouperation. No one to hold her hand, comfort her, encourage her during those lonely days in the hospital. Or afterwards.

He'd wanted to but because he was guarding her and training her, he'd needed to be firm, indifferent, detached. More than once she'd called him cold, hard-hearted, insensitive and inhuman.

Instead, he'd provoked, angered and nagged her as he coached, trained and drilled her to hone her body, build up her confidence, belief in herself. Prove she was resilient. Invincible like the diamond she is.

When she'd become stronger – more to prove to him she could do it – he knew his feelings had changed. He'd admired her determination to succeed, was fascinated by her free spirit. Cherished the infrequent moments when she beamed with delight, amusement and friendliness.

He knew he needed to let her fly, find the happiness she deserved so he persuaded her father to give her the independence to have a life of her own. He'd encouraged her to design the house, helped her move. Now protected and defended from afar.

He had heard Hayley's restlessness and Murdock's whimpers from his bedroom, but the ping on his cell phone alerted him to her movement from the bed. He understood why she stared forlornly into the darkness. Was sure Savannah's murder triggered tonight's dreams and would continue to do so for months to come.

Jaws clenched; his hands tightened into fists that wanted to pound Ortiz for once again putting her in this position. Intruding in her life.

It had taken over a year after Judith Toliver's murder for the dust to settle. Months of rehab, the trial, then training to build up her strength. Adjusting to being on her own, alone, not seeing her father.

He'd witnessed more than one of her nightmares via the cameras and always worried that he'd never been able to offer comfort.

He knew she hadn't had any dreams these past six months and wondered if her newest book had finally exorcised it from her memory. He'd read the galley, almost felt every blow she delivered to the victim.

He backed further into the shadows when Hayley turned, returned to the bed. He didn't want her to know he was aware of the nightmares. She wouldn't appreciate him knowing how the murder still affected her.

He knew he couldn't console her. Not now anyway. She wouldn't want it.

It aggravated him that Hayley should have to relive it all over again. Once again, her life would be an upheaval of emotions and intrusions.

She didn't deserve any of it.

Chapter Two

"Funny, I have another customer that buys these same pavers," James Fitzhugh, owner of *Green Mountain Hardware and Supply* commented as he handed Liam his receipt. He chuckled. "Ten at a time. With their size and weight, she can stack only so many in her car."

Average height, slender frame, long narrow face, his long thinning silver-gray hair gathered into a ponytail at the base of his neck with a leather cord, James pulled the loaded metal wagon. Followed Liam across the gravel parking lot to his truck.

"Hope she doesn't come back soon," he mumbled, "you bought all I had."

A smile tugged at Liam's lips. "I'm sure she'll understand." He'd found Hayley's plans for the patio and decided it would keep him busy for a few days. He'd plotted and leveled the area and laid the base sand.

James shook his head. "Not so sure. I mean, she's easy on the eye but I'm willing to bet underneath all that red hair is a fiery temper."

"Red head, huh," Liam grunted as he stacked a concrete square. "She come here often?"

Liam decided maybe he needed to find out how well Hayley had blended in the community.

James shrugged a shoulder. “Not so much in the beginning,” he handed Liam another square, “but she’s warming up.”

“Warming up? Sounds like she’s a little prickly.”

“I wouldn’t say prickly. Guess it’s cause she’s a loner. Never see her with anyone. Whole town was talking about her when she first moved here.” James continued to pass the blocks to Liam. “They’d already been talking about the big mystery house being built in the mountains. Then she popped up.”

“She moved into the house?” Liam wondered how familiar the town was with the location of her house. Was certain no one had trespassed during the construction as he had a crew camped out on the site the entire time.

“I guess. No other place for her to be. The construction was done, and she showed up out of the blue. Didn’t say a word to anyone. Took care of her business, then disappeared till the next time.”

“But she’s warming up?” Liam prompted.

“Yeah. After two years she’s smiling some. Don’t see her that much personally, but I understand she’s at the Farmer’s Market a lot.”

"Got an address?” Liam inquired. “Maybe I ought to check her out.”

James hesitated, wondered if maybe he was being a little too friendly. He didn’t know the woman but didn’t want to send trouble her way either.

“Just kidding,” Liam smiled as he put the last of the pavers next to cinderblocks, four-by-four boards, shovel and rubber mallet. He’d also checked Hayley’s tool shed, discovered she was organized but hadn’t thought the process through.

"Hope you're restocked before she comes back," Liam closed the tailgate, waved as he turned toward the front of the truck to leave.

He broke out in a grin as he imagined the townspeople talking about their reclusive member of the community. It pleased him that Hayley had warmed up to the town and they were giving her the privacy she needed.

She wouldn't relish the idea of him taking over her project, but he'd face that battle when he got back to the house. The rate they were going, he'd have the project finished before she noticed.

He'd been here two days and all they did was circle one another. She stayed in her office writing. He read a book, cleared brush in the woods, took Murdock with him for their morning runs, did his own security work at the dining room table.

Murdock was the only one that interacted peacefully with them.

She'd said she wouldn't cook for him, but he'd cooked for her.

He knew she didn't eat breakfast, simply walked across the hall to her office in the bedroom that faced the front drive. So, he'd ignored her, fixed his own breakfast, went about his business.

Found the fixings for a pot of beef and vegetable soup. She didn't have much else in the cabinets though.

He remembered she wasn't a junk food addict like him and had made the grocery store his first stop of the day. He'd picked up a roast and his favorite snacks – chips, crackers, peanuts, peanut butter, popcorn. Added her favorite chocolate bar and ice cream as consolation for when she discovered what he'd done with the patio.

It worried him she hadn't hit the gym in the basement yet. Figured she was deliberately burrowing in her office to ignore him. If things were going to heat up as he suspected, she needed to keep in shape so she could defend herself. He'd start hounding her about that before the end of the week.

On the drive back to the house, he decided he'd put the roast in the oven before unloading the truck. Let it simmer while he started a preliminary setup of the patio.

Since she was still holed up in her office, he whistled for Murdock to join him outside.

Haley smiled as her fingers raced across the keyboard. She'd made the front bedroom her office since it faced the drive. Gave her the perfect lookout for intruders that might wander in past the gated entrance, warning if she needed to seek protection. It also offered a simple view to stimulate thinking through an idea, plotting scenes, or outlining the story line.

The mystery was beginning to come together, and she didn't want to lose her momentum. She wrote by the seat of her pants, knew the ending but liked to let the story and her characters evolve on its own. She tracked her words and chapters, reevaluated the story midway through.

Right now, she was enjoying creating her characters, giving them their voice, backstories, establishing them within the plot.

A concerned co-worker discovered the murdered victim when she'd failed to show up for work two days in a row. Faith, her protagonist, has just earned her detective badge and is assigned the case. She became a cop because her mother was murdered when she was a child and it was still a cold case as they never found her mother's murderer. Faith would be in seventh heaven except rich kid Kyle has also been assigned to the case. Faith prefers to work alone and is in a constant state of aggravation because Kyle tends to always be late for meetings, interviews, the initial investigation.

Hayley's mouth curved into a smile. She wondered if she was basing the story on her current situation – the antagonism between her and Liam. Projecting her own feelings for Liam into her story.

Normally, when the muse flowed, Hayley worked to the point of exhaustion. Even Murdock had learned to only disturb her when necessary – outside for potty, food when hungry.

She didn't eat breakfast but had a Keurig in her office and had continued her routine of writing non-stop fueled with the caffeine while the ideas flowed. She straightened her back, shifted her shoulders left and right, up and down as she worked the kinks out of her taut muscles. Decided maybe she'd calm her jittery nerves with a jog while she pondered future plot ideas.

Liam had been here two days and she'd done her best to ignore him, but it was hard not to acknowledge when another person was in your space. Even if she was upstairs and he was downstairs.

Her body had always been attuned to his, no matter whether they had trained, travelled, argued or just avoided one another. She had enjoyed two years of not having him taunting, baiting or pushing her to keep up her self-defense training.

Despite the fact he'd been out of her life, she always felt as if he was looking over her shoulder no matter how alone she was.

No, there was no way she could completely ignore Liam Walker. She had sensed his presence when he discreetly checked on her from time to time, peeked over his laptop when she had dashed down for a quick snack.

She tried to ignore him when he walked the woods in front of the house, began clearing brush and branches that had fallen in storms. Squinted her eyes at him when he proceeded to load the debris into the bed of his truck; had no idea where he took it.

Yesterday, she'd breathed in the scent of the delicious soup, then was amazed to find a bowl with a sandwich on the credenza to the right of her desk. Decided she must have been wrapped up in a scene for him to sneak that past her.

Last night, she'd worked until eight in the evening. When she reached the point of exhaustion, was sure her brain couldn't come up with a word much less a sentence, she'd almost crawled down the stairs to find him relaxed on the sofa in the living room, reading a book. He ignored her of course and when she stepped into the kitchen, she found the note on door to the microwave informing her the plate of spaghetti and meatballs needed to be zapped sixty seconds.

She'd watched him leave earlier that morning, assumed he went to town. He had returned over an hour ago. Appreciated that he wasn't the 'honey I'm home' type of guy and had steered clear of her office. She checked the corner of her office, discovered Murdock's empty bed. Realized her dog had been spending too much time with Liam.

She leaned back in her chair and swiveled it from side to side, clasped her hands behind her head as she stared out the window. It occurred to her she'd had her fill of writing for a while and missed hugging the dog, badgering the man.

Since the sun was shining and it looked like a nice day outside, she decided maybe she'd go on that jog. She documented her progress on the manuscript, grabbed her notebook, and headed for the stairs. Maybe she'd work a little more on her patio project after her jog. Think about the story, make notes when inspiration hit.

Hayley stepped onto the back deck, stared down at Liam, kneeling on the ground, working on her patio project.

"What are you doing?" She demanded, hands on her hips.

"Finishing your project." His back to her, Liam thought he could feel the pricks of the angry sparks he was sure shot from her furious eyes.

"*My* project," she grumbled, descending the steps. "My *thinking* project. Whenever I need to think something through, I come out here and work on it."

"Sorry, I needed something to do. Thought I could help." He situated another paver.

Hayley studied the arrangement of the pavers. "That's not the way I wanted it."

"It's the only way the design will mesh."

"It's not the way I wanted it," she repeated.

"Fine." He sat back on his heels; settled gloved hands on his upper leg as he looked up, his narrowed brown eyes challenging her. "Show me."

She squatted, nudged him aside, began re-arranging the pavers but kept running into problems. Quickly realized she wasn't going to have enough pavers. Then she spied the second pile of pavers stacked in the yard.

"Where did those come from?"

"I bought them this morning. You didn't have enough. Figured I'd get them before someone else did. Lucky for you I bought the last of the inventory."

"Between the weight and size of the pavers, I could only get so many in my car." She defended herself.

"Yeah, the guy mentioned it. Said he'd be ordering more."

"How much do I owe you?"

Liam shrugged a shoulder.

"I don't want you paying for this."

"We can settle it later." Liam conceded.

"What are these blue ones?" She asked when she spied the smaller, narrower pavers.

"I thought it might add a little pop to the design. If you'd let me finish my design," he stated with a clipped voice, "you'll see how they square the corners."

Hayley ignored his suggestion, studied her design, shifted a few pavers, inserted the navy ones.

Liam restrained the smirk as he stood, moved to lean against the deck railing; appreciated her tight backside as she continued laying out her design. Figured she needed the exercise after sitting so long behind the laptop. Maybe he'd navigate her into the gym for a workout later.

When he understood, and approved, her design, he eased in, began setting the next row behind her.

"You know, you could make it a little bigger and add a firepit," he suggested after a few minutes.

"I'm in the middle of the woods," she grumbled, "why would I want a firepit?"

"Cool nights. Bundle up with a blanket. Hot chocolate. *Thinking* time."

"Smoke. Hauling ashes. Replenishing the wood pile," she retaliated.

She worked her way to the edge of the first row, discovered a scrap of paper beside the stack of pavers. *Kitchen. Stove. Grill.*

"What's this?"

"Ideas. You could also put in an outdoor kitchen."

Hayley shook her head. "All I want is a little corner where I can think. Sit at my bistro table and chairs. Have a cup of coffee in the morning; glass of wine in the evening."

"Just think what you could do if you added a grill. Outdoor kitchen."

"Why would I want to cook outside?"

"Company. Smoker. Enjoy the fresh air while entertaining."

"My current lifestyle doesn't include friends or company. Smoker sounds dangerous. No friends, no one to entertain." She stood, stepped past him.

"Leave my project alone." She growled before grabbing another paver to set it in the row behind him.

They began to work quietly, consistently. She tried to maintain a distance, but they inadvertently bumped shoulders or backed into one another from time to time. Once, they reached for the same paver at the same time. It amazed Hayley that she felt the jolt of shock up her arm through the thick gloves.

Liam frowned at the electrical charge that thrilled throughout his body. He raised his hands, backed off to give her the space to grab her block. Couldn't understand how they had trained hand to hand combat, and he'd never experienced the quivers before.

He found himself very cognizant of her movements. Chuckled to himself when he sometimes heard her talking to herself as she concentrated on placing the blocks, pause from time to time to scribble in her notebook.

Two hours later, they had the area set. Hayley stood back and studied it. Discovered it was twice the size she had intended but offered her enough room for a table and chairs, separate conversation area. And maybe a grill, she acknowledged to herself.

"What's that?" She pointed to the stack of cinderblocks and four by four Douglas Fir boards.

"My bench and planter idea. For the corner over there." He pointed to the far side of the patio closest to the woods.

She watched him stack eight of the blocks, two blocks on each level to make four levels, turning the blocks on their sides on the third level. He did the same four feet away then situated the boards side by side within the holes on the third level to form a seat.

"Now you have a bench and can buy some blue and yellow flowers to put in the holes of the top row there."

"Humph," Hayley responded.

Liam's lips twitched when she grabbed her notebook, climbed the steps to the back door. Turned to study the bench one more time. Imagined she would be stewing about which flowers to purchase the next time she went to the Farmer's Market in town.

The scent of pot roast, onions and garlic wafted throughout the house when they stepped inside.

"Dinner should be ready in a couple hours if you want to work on your notes, get cleaned up before eating."

"Okay, thank you."

Liam's brows knitted as he studied her when she headed up the stairs. He'd expected an argument or refusal. Not a thanks.

He plugged the USB flash drive into the computer, studied the copied emails the Hughes woman had sent and received over the last year. Some were gloating. Most bragging about how hard she worked.

He looked for the ones from Jillian McLeod. Snarled as he examined them over and over. Big help they were. No comments. No addresses. Just file after file, after file.

He jumped up with such a force, the chair almost overturned. Jammed his hands in the pockets of his pants and paced.

The Hughes bitch was dead and never spilled a word about where the Turner woman had relocated. The whole fucking murder was a wasted effort. He didn't know any more than he did in the first place.

He'd followed the story of the murder online. Found the woman's obituary. Searched for any pictures from the funeral but found none. No mention of Gerard Turner who had somehow hidden his darling baby girl from the world. No mention of the bitch's relationship with Hayley Turner. Just praised her writings as Jillian McLeod.

He wasn't an idiot. He knew the Hughes bitch was a front for Jillian McLeod. Hayley Turner was the brains behind the books.

The news article mentioned she had the new book coming out. It grated that she was making all this money at his expense.

Kramer said they were getting close. They'd have an address soon. Well, he was tired of waiting to hear from the crew. How long did it take to study IP addresses? Unravel the re-routed emails.

Cold eyes stared into the dark night.

He wanted the Turner woman found. She had to pay.

Chapter Three

"I talked to your father earlier this evening," Liam replenished Hayley's glass with the last of the malbec wine.

They had both showered, changed and were seated at the kitchen table after dinner.

Liam, dressed in clean jeans and sweatshirt, had had to take an extra gulp of his wine when a barefoot Hayley skipped down the steps in her black stretch twill pants and ash rose colored boyfriend shirt. The hem of the pants hugged her small ankles, accenting her long slender legs, the shirt ended just past her bottom. Her luscious dark auburn hair hung loose; the diamonds of her necklace sparkled from the unbuttoned opening just above the cleavage of her breasts.

He'd felt as if he'd just come up gasping for air after being taken down by a sudden ocean wave. He frowned, concerned that she should all of a sudden have this effect on him. Decided his immunity to her charm had mellowed during his absence and he needed to tread carefully if he was going to do his job.

"He attended Savannah's funeral today. Expressed your condolences. They understood why you were unable to attend."

"I still should have been there." Hayley stared into her wine glass. "I'm not a good friend."

Thankful that he'd held off on this conversation until after dinner, Liam tossed a sympathy card onto the table. "Sign this, write a note. Anything."

"And how will I deliver it to them without divulging my location?"

"Just do it. I'll see that the family gets it."

She heaved a heavy sigh. She didn't need to be taking her frustrations out on Liam. Not after he had helped her regain control of her life after Judith's murder and the attack; taught her self-defense. Gave her the freedom to have an independent life.

Not after he'd helped her with the patio today.

"How is he? My father? I miss him. I haven't seen him in five years."

"He's good. I don't see him as much either. He misses you as well. Is worried with these latest events." Liam leaned back in his chair, twirled the stemless glass on the table. "Hayley, your father loves you very much and is in constant fear for your safety. More so now. We still don't know what Savannah might have told her killer."

"I know. I remember my mother telling me a parent never stops worrying about their child. Well," she slid Liam a despondent look, "the same can be said for the adult child. After what happened to my mother, I can't help but worry about my father. He's all I have and is in just as much danger as I am."

Liam thought about Hayley's mother. He'd never met Julia Turner but learned of her charismatic charm and generosity from her husband and colleagues that had worked with her. He knew Julia worked beside her husband, had been involved in the community, supported charities, attended fundraisers.

She had been killed in a freak accident twelve years ago – lost control of the car and driven off the side of a mountain. Had been missing two days before they found her.

Hayley had been sixteen at the time. Impressionable age to lose her mother. He'd been told they were close and she took her mother's death very hard.

Hayley glanced around her. "I guess this house is the closest I've come to having a real home. A sense of privacy. At least I don't have the security guards around all the time."

Liam grimaced. Felt guilty about the interior cameras she was unaware of. Wondered what she would say when she realized she didn't even have that privacy.

"You were never one for having someone hovering over you," Liam agreed. "I guess this is the best we could do. At least you have your space and time for writing."

"Maybe," Hayley nodded her head, her soft green eyes studying him over the rim of her glass as she sipped her wine. It occurred to her this may be the longest complacent conversation they'd had in a while. Wondered if they could ever have a conversation without it turning into an argument.

"I take it you've started a new book?" Liam decided to enjoy the pleasant chat. Not the usual, snippy comments as they circled one another.

Hayley bobbed her head again. Contemplated whether she should let on he was the model for Kyle.

"Do you mind if I ask, where you come up with the plots for your murders? With six books, you ought to be out of murder scenarios by now."

"There's always *what if*. For instance, a couple weeks ago, we had a plane crash into the side of the mountain. I couldn't help wondering what if one of the passengers was the President. Or some corporate executive?

"Or a prison inmate that had escaped from jail and managed to survive the crash. Was living in the woods and started murdering women that resembled his mother.

"What if a husband rewrote his will to include his mistress, then is murdered. Who did it? The wife or the mistress?

"What if William Ortiz met with an unhealthy ending in prison? Would anyone try to find who did it? Would anyone even care?"

Hayley took another sip of her wine, studied Liam with smoldering sultry eyes. Thought about the fact her sex life was non-existent.

What if Liam Walker stood, took her in his arms, kissed her senseless, flickered through her thoughts. Hayley jerked, could feel her cheeks grow warm. Decided the wine must be affecting her more than it should.

Liam contemplated the transformation, was intrigued with her control as she stood, drained and rinsed the glass, set it on the counter.

"What about your characters? Do they materialize in your mind? Or do you think of anyone in particular?"

Hayley cleared her throat as she returned to the table, tucked a leg beneath her as she pinched off the corner of a brownie, tossed it into her mouth. "You were actually my first victim."

Liam's eyebrows rose, his lips twitched. "Somehow, I'm not surprised."

He remembered the tension they experienced during their earlier hand to hand combat days together. She'd been weak at first but caught on fast. She was also tenacious about her independence; didn't want anyone following her around, telling her what to do.

"You were training me. Always demanding more. Taking me down non-stop."

"If I hadn't, you wouldn't have learned. Gotten stronger. Your father wouldn't have let you have this place on your own."

"I know that now, but at the time-" She recalled the bruises, constant humiliation. Frustration at the lack of alone time.

"Hayley, it hasn't been easy for me either. I've lost count of the times you managed to elude your guards. Your father was always calling me. That's why he assigned me to you full time. He appreciated your wanting your independence, so he put me in charge of your training, the construction of your house. And when you couldn't settle on this property or kept changing the house plans, I had to coordinate everything."

Hayley's eyes grew round. She'd had no idea that Liam had any part of the project. Thought it was her father. She made a circular motion with a finger to entail the house. "*You* did all this?"

Liam nodded. "Your father figured it was best if you didn't know. Considering I wasn't your favorite person at the time."

Hayley recalled the friction and tension in the early days of the house project. She was still getting used to having him in her life. Hated the fact that he didn't hesitate to express his opinions about the house she'd designed, properties she'd considered. Places she wanted to live. It occurred to her their conversation was about the turn.

"Are you the reason some of the properties fell through?"

Liam looked heavenward. Here we go, he thought.

"You were, weren't you," she slammed a palm on the table. So loud, Murdock lifted his head, whined softly.

"I had to consider the lay of the land, visibility." Liam defended himself. "The one by the ocean? It was too open, easy for people to infiltrate at night."

"Like this place is any different? I'm surrounded by woods. Anybody could be out there watching the place. Observing my every move." Her jaw clenched. "Are you why the realtor kept suggesting this place?"

He cast her a veiled glance. "Can you honestly say you haven't been happy here? Would you have been able to write more by the ocean, in the big city? You must admit it gives you more privacy. Trails for exercise, alerts should anyone get past the gates. Solitude for all those *thinking* walks you take."

"How do you know about my *thinking* walks?"

Liam tucked his head, shook it. The evening was going downhill fast. Maybe it was time she was informed about the cameras. Or maybe it would be best if they didn't talk to one another. His grave of guilt kept getting deeper and deeper.

"Hayley, do you think your father, or I would give you so much independence without some assurances in place? That you would be safe."

"You trained me."

"That still needs to be determined. I haven't seen you working out since I got here."

"I have the security system."

"Yes, but we needed other precautions as well."

"Other precautions? As in...cameras?"

Liam nodded his head.

Hayley studied him, then jumped up. "You have cameras in my house?" She accused.

“Not the bathroom,” he stated, “and only on the window in your bedroom.”

Hayley turned white. Her bed was beside the window. She realized he probably had a good view of her restless, sleepless nights when the dreams haunted her. She wondered if he could hear her cries.

“It’s the principal of it,” she accused, an edge in her voice. “It’s an invasion of my privacy.”

“It’s not like I watch you all day,” he defended himself.

Just every hour or so, he thought to himself.

"To be sure you’re okay. Movement triggers the camera, which triggers the app on my phone. I check in, be sure everything is okay.”

“I’m sure you quickly discovered that my life is dull. No action. Or visitors.”

Liam shrugged a shoulder. “There were a couple times I almost came. Once, a couple months ago, there’d been no movement and all the screens were gray. I did worry then. Everything was dark. Then I caught the glow of the computer monitor, looked closer, could barely make out your shape. If it weren’t for the movement of your fingers, I would’ve worried. Guess you were so wrapped up in your writing you hadn’t thought to turn the lights on.

“I watched you for over an hour. When you came out of your zone, you turned the lights on, then went to bed. Thought it was odd you worked in the dark, then slept with the light on. Figured you must have scared yourself.”

Hayley remembered that night. She was working on a murder scene, reliving what happened to her, transferring it to paper. Was surprised when she finished the scene, realized how dark the house had gotten. The scene had been so gripping, so vivid.

“Who do you think monitors the front gates? Gets the calls if there are intruders? You are hours away if the wrong person learns where you've relocated. I needed some notice if someone managed to trespass onto the property."

"You have them in the woods as well?"

Liam nodded his head. "We've been lucky so far, but things might be different from now on. We don't know what Savannah said before she died."

"The day Judith died was the day I lost my independence." "Hayley shook her head in frustration. "It has always been about what you and my father want. Well, what about me?" She paced to the door to the deck. "What about my privacy? What I want?"

She pivoted, raced up the steps.

Hayley tried to scream but nothing would come out. Her heart pounded, body shook uncontrollably as she hugged herself, tried to call for help but the words wouldn't come.

She felt her legs tighten as she tried to run but couldn't move. Yet she felt weak, exhausted as if she'd been running from everything.

Cameras were everywhere, flashing in her eyes, blinding her. Videoing her lack of movement.

Her world moved at a breakneck speed as eyes of all shapes and sizes twirled around and around her, causing her to be dizzy as they watched her, judged her, mocked her efforts to get away.

She threaded her fingers through her hair, covered her ears, tried to block out the loud booming voices that shouted at her. Jeered her.

She peered over her shoulder, worried he would catch her.

"You'll never be free of me," she heard him scream. "I'll always find you no matter where you hide."

She felt so isolated. So tired.

"Liam," she called out.

Her chest hurt; she reached up to feel the necklace around her neck. Her hand cupped it and she experienced a calmness.

Liam leaped out of the bed, sprinted around the corner into her bedroom. His stomach was rock hard from the shock of hearing Hayley's frantic, piercing cry for help. She'd never called out to him like that.

His heart pounding, he stared down at her white face, still wet from the tears of the nightmare. It appeared the terror had passed so he pulled the cover over her still shivering body, saw the hand that clasped the necklace.

Murdock leaned against him, rested his head on the bed next to Hayley's hand.

Liam straightened, brushed his hands through his hair then down his face as he tried to steady his heart.

The nightmares seemed to be escalating and it angered him that she would never be free of them until Ortiz was six feet under.

"Found her." A gruff voice announced on a cell phone one thousand miles away.

Chapter Four

Hayley jogged down the trail. Her black yoga pants, black racerback tank top and black running shoes matched her mood. Angry, enraged and furious. Same as her protagonist who was trying to solve a murder with an obnoxious rich kid partner.

She hadn't slept well and was still unsettled from the nightmare. It had been so different, so disturbing and she blamed Liam for it. All that talk about cameras was so unnerving.

All she wanted to do was escape with her writing. She was trying to draft Faith and Kyle's story and needed her alone time to do so. Things had been going so smoothly until Liam arrived and turned her life upside down. Yesterday's joy that the story was coming together had evaporated after her argument with Liam last night. She'd tried to work on it some more, but the muse just wasn't there.

Then the nightmare had shattered what was left of the night. She'd drifted in and out of dreams, thought she sensed Liam's presence at one point. She'd awakened early, knew she should be writing about Faith's dealing with Kyle, but she needed to work off the frustration from last night.

Probably should have done so in the gym downstairs instead of outside in the first light of dawn.

She also felt guilty about her accusations that Liam and her father had stolen her independence. Her privacy. She realized her father was concerned for her safety, wanted what was best for her and was confident Liam would get the job done but not at the price of her personal space.

And she had to admit she liked the location of the house, agreed with Liam's reasoning about the other properties but it would have been so much better if this property had been her idea.

Hayley stopped, leaned forward, her hands resting on her knees as she tried to catch her breath.

Wasn't it her idea? She scolded herself. Didn't she make the final decision?

She still wasn't happy about the cameras. Liam said he had monitored her work at her computer. She tried to envision her office and had no idea where any camera might be installed that she wouldn't have detected it.

She vowed that before the end of the day she would make him show her the location of every one of the cameras that spied on her. Then she'd flip him the bird next time she was mad at him.

And what about the woods, she fumed as she glanced up, squinted her eyes through the towering trees. Where were those cameras? How many were there? She couldn't imagine the cost, and planning, that went into the project for this overextended security.

Hayley jumped when Murdock raced past her. She had specifically left him in the house because she wanted to be alone. That meant Liam was aware she was outside the house.

Her jaws clinched, lips formed a firm pout, she jogged after the dog. Wondered if Liam would be racing by her next.

Or would he hold back? Be happy with following, maintaining his pace, doing his job as he called it.

Or he might be angry enough to tackle her from behind. She bared her teeth, imagined the enjoyment of giving Liam Walker a rough tumble in the woods. Showing him she was capable of handling anything he wanted to dish out.

Liam was waiting for her when she slid the back door open twenty minutes later. Brows knitted, intense brown eyes narrowed, lips pressed in a straight line, arms crossed over his chest, he leaned against the kitchen counter.

"Feel better," he snarled.

After being awakened by her blood curdling scream, he'd spent the rest of the night listening to her toss and turn. He'd finally drifted off at five and hadn't appreciated the phone alert when she left the house giving him no inkling she intended to do so. It was all he could do to let the pacing Murdock out the door to follow her.

Still breathing hard, sweat trickling down her spine, Hayley moved to step past him.

"Not so fast," he grabbed her elbow, guided her toward the basement stairs.

"I've tried to be patient," he nudged her ahead of him down the steps. "Given you your space. You think you're so fit? So strong? Let's see how well you can protect yourself. Next time you get frustrated, work it off in the gym," he ordered, giving her one last shove at the bottom of the steps.

Hayley turned on him as soon as her feet hit the concrete floor. Put all her weight into the fist she aimed at his chin.

Liam expected it and deflected in time, but not before feeling the force of air that followed her swing. Velocity was good, he reflected to himself.

He caught her over his shoulder, took three long strides and dumped her on her rear onto the oversized mat. Stepped back studied her through squinted eyes. On guard. Ready for her next attack.

"It was on the tip of my tongue to apologize," Hayley made the pretense of struggling up off the mat, "but now... not so much."

Liam grabbed the foot that aimed for his crotch, yanked it up so she lost her balance, landed flat on her back.

Ouch, Hayley groaned to herself when the back of her head bounced against the mat.

Hands up, his palms facing him, Liam bent his fingers, encouraged her next move.

Her cheeks pink with frustration, Hayley ignored the slight pain to her tailbone, bared her teeth as she jumped up, aimed right and left punches at his face which he averted with his arms. She angled a hard punch for his solar plexus but hit his firm stomach instead. Her mouth curved at the sound of his grunt.

Liam continued to dodge her next two fists before hooking a foot around the back of her ankle and lifting it, threw her off balance.

Before falling, Hayley grabbed one of his ears with one hand, his shirt with the other, and pulled him with her. They both landed on the mat, Liam on top. Breathing hard, her teeth bared, she bucked beneath him tried to knock him off, but he used his weight to scrunch her, his hard body pressed her further against the mat.

Hayley experienced a momentary lapse of fear when he trapped her legs beneath his, her wrists above her head with a hand. She couldn't budge him, and it brought back memories of their earlier training days when he always had her at a disadvantage.

She hated being dominated. Being trapped and unable to escape.

Liam gripped her jaw with his free hand, held her face in place as he stared down at her, recognized the alarm in her quick gasp and dilated pupils. Their faces inches apart, his brows knitted, nostrils flaring, his eyes rotated between her eyes and mouth. He was uncomfortable with the way his body responded to the soft breasts that pressed against his chest with each hard breath she took. Angry that he is aroused by her slim firm body that wiggled beneath his. Annoyed with his hardness nestled against her hip.

They both held baited breaths, wondered who would make the next move.

Hayley worried she had pushed him too far. Her stomach muscles tightened, she is very aware of his firm muscles, inhaled the soap, pleasant clean aftershave.

"You're rusty," he grumbled before he jumped up, released her. "Tomorrow, we start our old routine." He marched toward the stairs. Needed to put some distance between them; time for his body to cool down.

Hayley leaped up, followed him up the stairs.

"I want to know where you put those cameras. Every. Single. One of them," she demanded, undaunted by the fact that he had defeated her, insinuated she was soft. She was more concerned about her privacy now.

Liam stepped into the kitchen, pointed to the crown molding over the back sliding doors; to the squared blocks with a floral design in the far corner.

Hayley stomped over to study it, saw the miniscule black center of the pattern. Turned to see that it was aimed toward the kitchen and garage door where Liam stood. He pointed to the same design above the garage door.

He marched around the refrigerator into the living room; aimed a finger at the molding above the arched opening between the kitchen and living room. Stepped aside when Hayley moved to stand in his spot, realized this camera scoped the steps going upstairs and the front door.

"There's one on the inside of the garage doors aimed at the kitchen door and the door to the back yard."

"What about my office?"

Liam climbed the stairs, aimed a finger at the one above his bedroom door that monitored the staircase. Stepped inside her office, indicated one in the corner of the door aimed at her desk and window, another in the corner above the window that tracked the hall, stairs and entrance to her bedroom.

"My bedroom?"

He marched across the hall, pegged the far corner of the room across from the double wide window that offered a view of the back yard.

Hayley stood in the corner, realized he couldn't see the entire bed, which was just beyond the window. But he would be able to watch restless movement if he searched hard enough. Meaning he was aware of her nightmares.

"Maybe my suspicions that you were always looking over my shoulder weren't too far off," she mumbled.

"I wasn't looking over your shoulder. Just checking in from time to time."

Liam cupped his hands around her shoulders, gave her a slight shake to make her look up at him.

"Red," Liam reverted to his nickname for her that tended to spout from his lips during times of frustration, "if your father had his way, you'd have round the clock guards. I appreciated you didn't want that. This was the only way he would agree to let you live this far away. The cameras enable me to do my job, report to him on a weekly basis. I knew you wouldn't like it which is why I didn't tell you. Until now."

He exhaled a deep breath, gave her another shake before dropping his hands.

"There's another precaution even your father doesn't know about. And I didn't tell you because then I'd have had to tell you about the cameras."

He pointed to the alcove where her bed was located.

"I don't know if you remember but the walk-in closet was supposed to be where the bed is. I flipped the design, put the closet on the outside wall."

He nudged one of the closet barn doors aside. Stepped inside the small walk-in, pushed a button on the underside of the shelf above the long metal rod holding her clothes.

Hayley jumped when the wall to her left shifted, and a pocket door opened to what looked like a dark stairwell. Liam reached around the corner to flip a switch that lit up a metal spiral staircase.

Her mouth fell open, amazed she hadn't discovered this on her own. Never questioned the wasted space from inside her bedroom. She stepped into the staircase, discovered a Glock and other handguns mounted on the wall to her left.

“They’re all loaded, ready for action,” Liam advised her.

Fifteen flat-screen monitors were mounted strategically on the corner walls that surrounded the steel steps. Upon closer inspection, Hayley realized many of the monitors were for the cameras within the house – in the kitchen, living room, her office – as well as the front gate and in the woods.

“I designed this so you wouldn’t be trapped upstairs. If someone had broken in, I would have called you, told you what to do. These monitors show you the location of anyone inside and outside the house.”

He reached for her hand, pulled her behind him down ten steps, pushed another button that opened into the pantry off the kitchen.

“If no one is in the kitchen, you can escape out the back door to the woods or to the garage and your vehicle.”

“But the stairs keep going down.” Hayley pointed out.

Liam continued down the stairs to the basement level where another button opened a door to a small room.

“Right now, it’s just a room, a shelter. My thinking was to dig a tunnel to the woods, but it would have taken too long, and I didn’t want you to be suspicious. I also didn’t want just anyone digging the tunnel, so I had to put it on the back burner until I had the time to coordinate things. Still not sure I want to pursue it.”

He flipped a light switch and pointed to more handguns and ammo on the shelves.

"It's good you’re not claustrophobic. I figured this room would give you a haven for a few hours until I arrived to rescue you.”

Hayley contemplated the concrete floor, solid bare walls and wooden box standing on end. The shelving cramped the space so it was little more than a large closet.

She imagined the room with the door closed and decided Liam had more faith in her than she did.

"Maybe it's good we haven't had to put this little room to the test. I'm not sure Murdock or I would be able to stay in here more than an hour before going stir crazy."

"You could if you knew someone was looking for you. Of course, I'd be in constant contact via cell phone." He stuffed his hands in the back pockets of his jeans, slanted a look down at her while he rolled back on the balls of his feet. "That is provided you had your cell phone on you."

Hayley patted her butt, waist and sports bra, realized in her haste to jog, she'd forgotten to bring her cell phone.

She threw her hands up in defeat.

"Okay, I may have been a little rash earlier. I'm sorry I lost my cool. And after seeing all this, I have to say I'm impressed. You put so much thought into this and I'm amazed I didn't know my house as well as I thought. I appreciate your effort to provide a haven for me."

Liam shrugged. "It's what I do. It's my job."

Later that morning, Liam hid Hayley's notebook beneath the log, scattered some leaves around it before heading back to the house to let the dog out. Besides training Hayley in self-defense, he worked with Murdock's search and rescue training. It was one thing for the dog to protect her from intruders, but he needed to know how to track her if they should become separated. God forbid Hayley should be kidnapped.

The Belgian Malinois breed was known for their exceptional sense of smell and precision tracking abilities and Murdock had proven to be superior in both skills.

Liam opened the door, clicked the timer, relaxed on the deck, and waited.

When he heard the ping of his app on his cell phone, he clicked on the picture, watched the car approach the front gate and stop. Liam leaned forward on alert as he studied the guy who exited the car – average height, stout, too far away to detect facial features – as he walked the distance of the brick entrance, touched the iron gate, shook it to determine if it was closed.

The guy wandered the perimeter, took his time studying the lay of the land. Stepped over to examine the aluminum weatherproof delivery box mounted on the concrete slab, next to the mailbox that was enclosed in one of the brick walls.

He debated walking down to the gate, confronting the man until the guy returned to his car, backed around the curve to the main road.

Liam shook his head; worried Hayley's hidden hideaway may have been discovered.

Chapter Five

Hayley set the ground beef and sausage on the counter, started chopping the onions and garlic. Smiled that the day that started on a bad note might end in her favor.

After discovering the location of the cameras and her secret chamber, she and Liam had called a truce. Hayley had showered and settled down to a productive morning of writing. Liam decided to take a nap.

Hayley stared at the monitor decided it was time for Faith and Kyle to call a truce as well. Found she enjoyed narrating their arguments, Faith's snide comments, Kyle's persistent bantering.

Faith began to appreciate Kyle's objective approach in their discussions about the case. Neither can understand why the victim's cell phone was missing; Kyle bet it is still in her apartment. Faith insisted the sweepers had searched and nothing, so Kyle pinged the number, discovered the blinking dot.

Hayley closed her eyes as she narrated Faith and Kyle arriving at the victim's apartment, discovering it has been ransacked. After meticulously searching the disarray, it occurs to Kyle they should have thought to call the number.

Where would the victim have hidden her cell phone, Hayley wondered. She stared into the woods outside the window, imagined different places she might hide something in her house. Looked up and eyeballed her spider plant. Her mouth curved into a smile; her fingers danced over the keyboard.

"Kyle jolted at the musical notes that sounded across the room," Hayley spoke as she typed. "He raced to the window, yanked the pot out of the macrame plant holder and grinned when he spied the *Ziplock* bag tucked between the clay pot and flat dish. My favorite dish is lasagna, he bragged to Faith as he held the still ringing cell phone up for Faith to see."

Hayley blinked, didn't know where the dish came from other than it was her mother's favorite, and she recalled the fun she and her mother had experienced preparing it together.

Maybe the readers might enjoy the recipe, she decided and made a note to include in the back of the book.

The more Hayley thought about the recipe, the hungrier she got so she'd suffered through a trip to town with Liam in tow to purchase the ingredients she didn't have on hand. Thankfully, Liam had stayed outside with Murdock when they returned.

While the beef, pork, onions and garlic browned and tenderized in the skillet, she started putting together the sauce – tomatoes, tomato sauce, parsley flakes, sugar, salt and basil leaves – then added it to the skillet.

Dashed upstairs to plot out the next scene while the sauce simmered for an hour.

She had just put the water on to boil for the noodles and was getting ready to mix the cheeses when Liam decided to come inside. Snitched a couple spoons of the cottage cheese before she added the parmesan cheese, parsley and oregano to the mixture.

He never spoke but reached into the cabinet above her for the jar of peanut butter, around her for the crackers from the basket on the counter, the drawer beside her for a knife. He settled on the other side of the bar to watch as she put the dish together – layer of noodles, meat sauce, mozzarella cheese and cottage cheese mixture – while fixing his snack.

Hayley knew her cheeks were flushed from the hot noodles and concentrating on preparing the layers. It unnerved her that he was watching her in silence.

"My protagonist lost a bet with her partner whom she doesn't like. He said he wanted a lasagna dinner." She plated a second layer of noodles, checked the recipe again to be certain the meat sauce was the next layer. "My mother and I used to enjoy making lasagna together, so I decided to add it to the story. Thinking about it made me hungry so I decided to make it. Planning to include the recipe in the back of the book."

"Why doesn't she like him? Your protagonist?"

"Because he's always in her way, like someone else I know," she glanced over at him. "He's a rich boy that doesn't need to work but has chosen to be a cop."

Hayley sprinkled the last of the mozzarella cheese from the package onto the sauce, scraped the remainder of the cottage cheese mixture from the bowl. Turned to toss the empty cheese bag into the trash on her way to the sink. Found the bag had disappeared, Liam reaching for the bowl. She frowned, leaned over to spoon the last of the sauce on top as he dabbed a finger into the skillet for a sample.

Liam threw his hand up and backed away when she glared at him. He studied the thirteen by nine-inch glass dish rounded a half-inch above the sides.

"That's an awful big dish, you planning to share?"

"I probably should have picked a simpler dish, but it freezes well. Yes, I'm going to share but I suggest you eat from that side of the dish." She pointed to his side of the dish then grimaced when she lifted what felt like five pounds of pasta, set it in the preheated oven.

"Why?"

"You keep getting in my way, I might sprinkle a little arsenic in the sauce," she stated as she marched out of the kitchen.

It was a matter of time before the truce ended and tempers flared. When she'd become so engrossed in writing down her frustrations with Liam to put in the book and plotting scenes for Faith to experience the same emotions with Kyle she realized she was overdue to take the lasagna out of the oven. She caught a whiff of the delicious aroma and raced down the stairs only to find Liam had already done so.

When she rubbed her hands together, decided to prepare the salad ingredients, she found he had not only diced everything but tossed it together, put the tomatoes in a separate dish . When she tried to season and slice the bread, he bumped elbows with her as he searched the drawer for the corkscrew, then proceeded to open the wine.

Hayley cast an exasperated look his way, wondered if he was being obnoxious on purpose.

"I'm keeping an eye on my side of the dish," he teased with a gleam in his eye.

The following morning, Hayley bounded down the steps, decided she'd have some of his fresh coffee rather than her bland Keurig brand.

"I just realized I haven't filled the birdfeeders for a couple days."

"Already done," Liam responded as he loaded his breakfast dishes in the dishwasher.

"But I like filling the feeders," she grumbled, disappointed he had interloped on one of her favorite chores.

"And you're out of birdseed. We also need more peanut butter. I ate the last of it yesterday. We can go to town later this morning."

"You can. I have work to do. Besides, we went to town yesterday. You should have gotten it then." She headed for the coffee pot.

"You never want me to go inside with you."

"Because I don't want the people talking about us. Where's Murdock? I haven't seen him all morning. Maybe I'll take him out for our jog."

Liam nodded to the dog dozing on his bed. "Sleeping, we went out while you were writing."

"We have a routine but lately, *my* dog seems to be spending more time with you."

Liam shrugged a shoulder. "You're always writing. Jealous?"

"Of course not," she exclaimed, "we had a routine and your being here has thrown a kink in things."

"What am I supposed to do? Ignore him?"

Before she could help herself to some coffee, he had poured it and was handing it to her.

Hayley squinted at him recalled their dinner preparation the night before.

"You would think with a house as big as this one, we wouldn't be under each other's feet all the time. You're always between me and where I want to go. I'm capable of getting my own coffee."

She pivoted, bounded back up the steps to her office.

Liam leaned against the counter, shook his head as she flounced out the room. He understood her frustration all too well. No matter how hard they tried to ignore it, the tension was always there. She didn't want him there; he was annoyed with his growing attraction.

After yesterday's volatile match in the basement, it occurred to him he was more aware of her than he should be. Not if he was going to protect her. He needed to be objective.

It annoyed him that those long legs, shapely hips, soft breasts, sharp tongue intrigued him so.

Hell, she didn't even have to be in the same room, he thought as his body throbbed.

No, the next time she challenged, argued or questioned him he might have to make her work off her anger with a good fight.

He hadn't told her about the visitor at the front gate. The possibility that her hideaway might have been discovered. He'd hoped to keep her in the dark a little longer, but maybe she needed to know trouble might be heading their way.

When she snapped at him for interrupting her train of thought later that afternoon when he slipped the dish of lasagna on her credenza, he knew she was still upset with him, looking for a fight, so he decided to egg it on. He encouraged Murdock into his bedroom, closed the door. Didn't need the dog interfering, he wouldn't understand.

"Maybe you need to be more perceptive, cognizant of my whereabouts. Appreciative of my gestures," he nodded to the still steaming lasagna. "After all, I am a guest in your home."

"Guest," she snarled. "Intruder is more like it."

"An intruder that left soup on her desk the other day and you never acknowledged it."

Hayley leaped out of her chair. "I ate it, didn't I?" She challenged, raised her chin, clenched her fists at her waist. "You want to be thanked for every little thing you do? I didn't ask for the soup."

"That's not the point. You were so engrossed in writing. I could have been anybody."

"So," she shrugged a shoulder. "I tuned you out. That's how I write. I didn't ask for you to be here. Didn't ask for my friend to be murdered. You've shown me my escape route. I can take care of myself now. I don't need you anymore." She moved her fingers as if they were walking. "You can just mosey on back to the big city now."

"Not possible. Number one, I work for your father, he decides when I leave. Number two, you *do* need me. You're isolated. How many friends have you made since moving here?"

"I'm isolated because you and my father wanted me isolated. And friends? *How* can I make friends? Everybody is suspect. If I do make friends, they have questions. I'd have to explain my isolation, assumed identity. Anonymous writing."

She paced away from him.

"I can't afford friends. I'm a walking disaster. Look at what happened to the two friends I had! Just go," she threw her hands up in the air in defeat. "I can take care of myself."

Liam bared his teeth, angry at the defeated tone of her voice, order for him to leave. He was having no part of either.

"We'll see how well you can take care of yourself." He grabbed some zip ties from his back pocket, forced her into the seat in front of the desk, bound her wrists together, her legs to the chair.

"Let's see if you can maintain your record escape time. You know where to find me."

He exited the room, let Murdock out of his bedroom, followed the dog down the stairs.

Hayley was shocked. Her mouth fell open when she looked down at her bound hands, tried to move her feet. Liam had caught her by surprise. She didn't think in time to clench her hands side by side with her palms facing down when he grabbed her. It would have been a matter of unclenching her hands, turning her wrists so they faced each other, wiggling her thumbs, then her hands loose from the tie.

Instead, he'd bound her wrist to wrist before hooking her ankles to the legs of the chair.

She gripped the end of the tie between her teeth to tighten it some then raised her hands over her head, brought them down to her stomach. Forcing her elbows going out, she snapped the tie open.

Next, she bent down, slipped a fingernail under the tiny bar of the lock on her leg; lifted the tab to release the tie. After freeing her other leg, she raced down the stairs, rounded the corner into the kitchen where she found Liam leaning against the bar, arms across his chest, feet crossed at the ankles.

Hayley was so angry all self-defense tactics flew out the window of her brain. Her long legs charged as she flew at him, arms flailing, open hands trying to pummel him, slap him down.

Recognizing her maniacal mood, Murdock backed away toward the back doors.

Liam jerked to attention, averted the blows then ducked his head, trapped her arms against her side with his, and held on tight. He felt her rapid heart pounding against his, heard the anger in her rapid breaths.

Blind fury vibrated through her body as Hayley tried to slam his head with hers. Liam lifted her off her feet, backed her against the door to the garage.

They both glared at each other, breathing hard.

Her feet dangling, Hayley squirmed tried to break his hold, but he tightened it.

"Put me down," she ordered, wisps of auburn hair that escaped the long braid surrounded her flushed cheeks.

"Not until you calm down," he warned, tightened his grip, pressed her harder against the wall.

Liam's eyes challenged her olive-green eyes. God, she was beautiful, he thought. Chin up in defiance, flushed cheeks, eyes blazing with anger. His eyes flip-flopped between her fiery eyes and sensuous mouth.

Not the kind of fight he had envisioned, he decided when he felt his body come to attention.

"I'm going to hell for this," he mumbled before he took hungry possession of her mouth. His tongue breached her lips, connected with hers, consumed the anger that flowed between them.

Hayley inhaled a deep breath, alarmed at the torrent of emotions that overwhelmed her in the span of minutes. Feelings that had been suppressed for so long. She was shocked at the sudden turn of events, alarmed with the way her body was reacting, blown away with the thoroughness of his probing tongue, and stunned that she didn't want him to stop.

They both moaned when he angled his head, deepened the kiss. Pressed his arousal against her middle.

Neither registered the buzzer that sounded from the monitor on the counter in the far corner of the kitchen.

They broke apart when Murdock barked loudly, stared in the direction of the front door.

Chapter Six

"It's Kyle." Hayley raced across the room, studied the picture on the monitor. "The UPS guy."

Liam shook his head and cleared his throat, tried to regain control of his raging body. He was uptight that he'd lost control and kissed her. Unnerved to discover he wanted more. Disturbed to realize one kiss wasn't going to be enough.

"You know the UPS guy's name?"

Hayley swallowed hard, tried to calm her heart that still raced in reaction to Liam's kiss and Murdock's warning bark. She shrugged a shoulder.

"Only by name. As many packages as I've received the past two years, it's expected. Sometimes, I think he's my only link with the outside world. I told him I work from home and don't want to be interrupted. I learned through the rumor mill in town his birthday is in April; left him a birthday card. Leave bottled water in the box during the summer, a fifth of *Maker's Mark* for Christmas.

"Hey, Kyle," Hayley pressed the speaker button. "Everything okay?" She studied the ebony face, chocolate brown eyes that stared into the camera and frowned. He usually had a bright smile for her.

"I have a package, sorry."

"Okay. You can leave it at the usual spot."

"I need a signature this time. Sorry. I can bring it to the house if you want."

Hayley continued to contemplate Kyle.

"Something's wrong," she whispered. "Kyle always has a smile for me."

Liam stepped behind her, studied the body language – tight grip on the steering wheel, stiff posture, squared shoulders, flat-lined mouth.

"Open the gate, tell him to come ahead." He sprinted to the door to the back deck. "I'll wait in the woods."

Hayley released the gate switch.

"Okay," she answered to Kyle. "I'll meet you outside on the front porch."

"Thanks. Again, I'm sorry."

Why was Kyle being so apologetic? Hayley wondered. Convinced something was off, she opened the drawer, grabbed the small handgun among the cooking utensils, nestled it in the small of her back. Grabbed the small can of mace tucked within her spice rack, tucked it in the pocket of her jeans. She had weapons of defense scattered throughout her house, available in any case of an emergency.

She reached for Murdock's collar. "C'mon boy, let's go find out what's wrong with Kyle."

Hayley listened for the sound of the truck's engine while waiting on the front porch. She wondered if Liam was able to find an inconspicuous spot to hide. Was his obsession to keep the immediate surroundings cleared of underbrush working against him. Preventing him from hiding from possible intruders.

Liam peeked around a large oak tree off the back corner of the garage. Watched the brown box truck navigate the final curve up to the house. Eyes squinted, he thought he caught the slight movement of a shadow standing behind the driver. As it came closer, he detected the silver glint of a handgun nestled in the side of the driver's neck.

Kyle pulled up to the far side of the garage doors, away from the front porch but remained in his seat.

Liam ducked behind the tree listened to a mumbling male voice, picked up the footsteps on the metal tread of the vehicle. Peeked around to see the second man backed down; recognized the guy from the day before at the front gate. He aimed his gun at Kyle, motioned the driver to lead him to Hayley and the front porch.

Liam hoped by now Hayley was aware there was indeed an intruder on the truck and would be able to handle Murdock who was already growling.

Kyle stepped down, stiffened when the intruder grabbed his collar, pressed the barrel of the gun into the middle of his back as they rounded to the front of the truck.

While the two men focused on Hayley and Murdock on the front steps, Liam sprinted to the corner of the garage, quietly stepped out behind them.

"Hey," Liam startled both men, delivered a swift, hard fist to the intruder's chin when he turned. Gave him another punch as the intruder fell to the ground.

"You okay," Liam asked Kyle who had banged his head against the front side mirror of the truck.

"I will be in a couple years," Kyle rested his head on his arm as he leaned against the side of the box truck.

Liam kicked the perpetrator's pistol away when Hayley joined them, her own pistol aimed at the intruder, Murdock by her side.

"You might want to give the Sheriff a call," Liam suggested to Hayley.

Sheriff Jackson "Jack" Collins parked his cruiser beside the brown box truck. Black eyes studied the group congregated around the front porch.

He recognized the woman from seeing her in town with her dog. Hadn't been introduced yet but knew from the scuttle butt the pretty lady tended to keep to herself. Noting the Belgian Malinois dog breed, he wondered if there might be a reason for that seclusion.

Jack studied Kyle Evans who sat next to Hayley on the front step, elbows on his knees, head in his hands. Not the usual delivery guy that always had a smile on his face, joke to share.

He wasn't familiar with the tall guy – dark hair, six feet, stern expression – throwing balls for the dog. Or the stocky guy with salt and pepper hair sitting on the concrete, leaning against the garage doors with his hands behind his back, legs stretched out in front of him, feet zip-tied at the ankles.

Jack's large square hand reached for his hat, perched it over his cropped military style salt and pepper hair as he stepped out of the car, adjusted his holster. A little stockier since his days as a New York detective, he kept in shape challenging his two teenage stepsons with karate and basketball.

"Rough delivery?" Jack asked Kyle.

Kyle looked up, tried to smile. "You might say that sir. Scared the- "he stopped, cast a guarded look in Hayley's direction.

"Want to tell me what happened?"

Kyle blew out a breath. "I pulled up to Ms. Cox's gate, was getting ready to put her package in the delivery box when that guy," he pointed a finger at the bound perpetrator, "jumped inside the truck. He had a gun, aimed it in my face. Told me to call the house, say I had a special delivery, then drive him in."

Kyle looked at Hayley. "I'm sorry, Ms. Cox, but there wasn't anything I could do."

Hayley put an arm around him, squeezed his shoulder with her hand. His use of her assumed name – Amelia Cox – another security precaution Liam had put in place, almost distracted her.

"I immediately suspected something was wrong," Hayley continued. "Kyle usually has a bright smile but today he was so serious. So apologetic. This is Liam Walker," she raised a hand to introduce Liam to the Sheriff. "Liam has been visiting and suggested I let him in. He snuck outside to monitor from the woods. Intervene if necessary."

Jack turned to Liam. "So, you surprised him."

Liam nodded, tossed the ball to Murdock. "I hid behind a big oak, other side of the garage. Watched as they drove up. Perpetrator here wasn't too smart. Figured if I could see him, she could see him as well. I hoped she could control Murdock. I let them get out, then greeted him with a couple fists to the chin."

Jack looked over to the bound man, saw the beginnings of a bruise on the right side of his face before turning back to Kyle.

"Kyle is there anything you want to add?"

"No sir, just that I'll be more careful, more observant from now on. Never had this happen before."

A corner of Jack's mouth lifted. "Never hurts to be cautious," he affirmed. "I'm sure you've got a lot of people waiting for their packages, I think that's all I need from you. You're free to go. If I have any more questions, I'll catch up with you in town."

Kyle jumped up, turned to Hayley before he left. "I certainly am sorry about all this, Ms. Cox. He isn't your stalker, is he?"

Hayley blinked in confusion, remembered the stalker story she had fabricated to explain her precautions with the gate. "Ah, no," she chuckled, "he's not my stalker. And I appreciate your subtle warnings."

She handed him an apple, bottle of water and kiss on his cheek. "Thank you."

Everyone appreciated Kyle's skill with reversing the big truck in a tight space, maneuvering it down the narrow drive.

Jack Collins turned to Liam. "You must have had some special training to take this guy down so quickly."

"Yes, sir. Afghanistan. Secret Service. Now private service."

Jack switched to Hayley. "Ms. Cox, I think you moved here about the time I was elected Sheriff two years ago?"

"Yes, sir. I work from home. Wanted some peace and quiet and have enjoyed it here."

"Up until today, I'd say you got your wish." Jack chuckled. "Kyle mentioned a stalker. Is that why you moved here?"

The corner of Hayley's mouth quirked up. "I may have gone a little overboard when I tried to explain why I didn't want him bringing my packages to the house."

Jack looked from Hayley to Liam, back to Hayley. "Any reason for the secrecy? Private security?"

"Ms. Cox had a spot of trouble a few years ago," Liam chimed in. "I work for her father who wanted his daughter protected. I stopped by here a couple days ago to check in."

"She must have put you to work. I recall seeing you outside the hardware store the other day."

Jack chuckled at their blank looks.

"This is a small town, son. Not much goes on that either I don't witness myself or am informed of by our curious town folks."

Liam smiled, leaned down to accept the ball from Murdock, tossed it into the woods. "Yes, sir, I finished a patio the other day."

Jack studied the intruder still leaning against the garage doors, his bruise expanding across his face. "Our friend here doesn't look to happy. Did you talk to him?"

"Asked the basic who, what, why questions but he's not saying much."

"I'll take him to town, process him, turn him over to the big guys. Maybe they can joggle a few answers. In the meantime," he pivoted back to Hayley, "you be careful, young lady. And let me know if there are any more problems."

Liam waited for Hayley to go up to her office before he stepped onto the back deck to make his call.

"*Connecting Associates*," the female voice with a strong Bronx accent answered. Florence Sunden would be seventy on her next birthday. She was short – half an inch short of five feet – had cropped gray hair and reminded everyone of their favorite grandmother. She'd been a secretary all her life and wasn't ready to retire. Started out in Gerard Turner's office, became his second hand, worked alongside his wife. When Julia Turner was killed, she found she couldn't return to the office that held so many memories for her. So, Gerard Turner had installed her in the small office space two blocks from her condo, put her in charge of distributing his correspondence.

"It's Liam, you have a minute," Liam got to the point.

"Sure thing, honey. Everything okay?"

"Not sure. I was wondering about you."

"Well, except for the false alarm the other night, everything's going hunky dory."

"False alarm?"

"Yes, I got a call around nine last night that the office had been breached but when I came in to check, nothing was out of place."

"Hmm," Liam stared at the patio, a worry line between his brows. As part of Gerard Turner's conglomerate, *Connecting Associates* was also Savannah's contact for packages to Hayley. Florence forwarded the packages to Hayley's assumed name at her Vermont address. "I need you to check something. Would you grab your file for Hayley Turner? Tell me when her last package was sent."

"Know for a fact I sent one last week but give me a minute" Liam listened to the tap as Florence put the phone down, metallic click of the file cabinet. "That's odd, her file is missing. I know I filed the invoice after I entered it on the computer."

"So, you're saying the file is gone? Not misplaced?"

"Honey, I run a shipshape office here. I'm looking at my computer and see I documented that I filed the invoice last week."

Liam winced at the accusation. "I'm not questioning it. We just had an incident here and I think our perpetrator may have been in your office."

Liam heard the sharp gasp. "Oh, I'm so sorry. I hope everything is okay."

"Yeah, for now. You might want to check your cameras though. If you find anything, please call me."

An hour later he set a glass of wine on the living room coffee table in front of Hayley.

"Guess we can assume Savannah's murderer found something," he stated.

Hayley frowned.

After Sheriff Collins had left, she'd tried to work but found herself shutting down instead. Between the earth-shattering kiss, Kyle's visit, her mind wouldn't focus. She'd paced her office, come downstairs to pace the kitchen, settled on the living room sofa to mope.

"I told you she didn't know anything. She didn't *want* to know anything."

"Doesn't matter," Liam sat in the chair across from her, his elbows on his knees, wine glass dangling from his fingers. "Her laptop was on the table next to her body. Whoever killed her could have searched it. Downloaded files, emails."

"But she never knew where I lived. Always sent any packages to another address that were forwarded to me. We only corresponded via email. Not even on the phone."

"I just got off the phone with *Connecting Associates*. They're the company that forwarded the packages. It seems their office was breached the other night. When I called to check in, she discovered your file was missing. I suggested she check her video cameras. She did, called me back. It's a little fuzzy but he fits the description of our UPS intruder."

Hayley took a healthy sip of her wine, leaped up to pace to the steps and back, took another sip of wine. "So, we can now assume they know where I live?"

Liam sat back. "Until this is resolved, we might want to look at relocating."

"No," Hayley blurted. "I will not run again. Liam, I refuse to let them control my life."

Liam frowned. He couldn't blame her, but it made things difficult for him. Especially when he was certain her father would be saying the exact opposite.

Hayley squirmed in the bed. She couldn't move her arms or legs, felt like the covers were strangling her.

She was cold, shivering from fear not the weather. Her breath burst in and out as she found herself backed against the wall, looking left and right for any escape route. She could feel the rapid beating of her heart in her chest, hear the beat pounding in her head.

Shadows surrounded her but she needed to escape before he found her.

She could see Judith crumpled on the floor in front of the man. Hear her fearful cries, pleading with the man not to hurt her anymore. Begging him not to shoot her. She caught a whiff of the man's sweat when he grabbed a fistful of Judith's hair, raised her head, aimed the gun at her temple.

Hayley sat upright in the bed, cried out when the loud gunshot shattered her dream. She wept loudly that the dreams wouldn't stop. That she had to view her friend's death over and over.

She fought against the arms that surrounded her, her body struggling to back away from the warm body that was so much stronger. She was fearful, knowing what would come next.

"Hayley...Red..." a familiar voice soothed her. "it's just me, Liam. Wake up, it's just me. You're okay," Liam murmured into her ear as he hugged her close.

He'd listened for her whimpers – expected it – but shot out of his bed when Murdock raced into his room as if asking for help.

The blood curdling scream shocked them both.

He'd found her twisting her body side to side, her arms and legs thrashing against the covers. Anger and grief filled his heart when he heard her wail. Anger at the bastard that had caused the turmoil; grief for the woman that didn't deserve any of it.

He rocked her, let her cry. When she calmed some, he leaned back to study her ashen white face, trembling lips that gasped for breath.

"It was just a dream," he whispered against her sweating forehead. He lay on the bed beside her, still holding her close.

Hayley continued to sob as she tried to steady her breathing. She wrapped her arm across his chest, nestled into his warmth and was lulled back to sleep by the hand brushing up and down her back.

What the fuck was wrong with the idiot? He fumed. His body tense and sweating, he paced as he cracked his knuckles in anger.

Would anything go right?

He pounded a fist into the palm of his hand. It should have been a simple get in, kill the broad, get out. He couldn't even get past the fucking delivery guy.

And what was Walker doing there? Last he'd heard Walker was keeping a distance from the bitch, watching the old man.

Cold, hard eyes stared into the darkness beyond the window.

What was it going to take to get the job done? What was it going to take to make the bitch pay?

Chapter Seven

Hayley paced the office, stared in awe at the monitor. The two thousand words she wrote yesterday had disappeared. She always documented her work, tracked the number of words written, updated her notes. With all that happened the day before, she may have forgotten to save things but was certain the computer would do it automatically.

When she glimpsed the *auto recovery* files, she worried. It had auto recovered the original not the edited, expanded file. She double-checked the list of files, nothing.

She couldn't believe that after regaining her momentum after yesterday's argument and fiery kisses, Kyle and the UPS invasion, and last night's nightmare from hell, her computer had frozen up.

It had already been a difficult morning. She'd awakened alone in her bed but remembered the dreams and Liam comforting her. Uncertain what to say, she'd escaped to her work. Figured she'd come up with a way to thank him without having to grovel too much.

She had typed the Lasagna recipe into a file that could be added to the final draft of the manuscript and managed to dictate two thousand words, bringing Faith and Kyle a tad bit closer. He was impressed with her cooking skills and she with his selection of wine. Nothing like a good meal and bottle of fine wine to loosen the tension, stimulate discussion on the case and establish the beginnings of a working relationship.

And now her computer decided to be difficult.

Hayley began pounding the keyboard with all ten fingers at once. Jumped up in frustration when nothing happened; threaded fingers through her hair while the chair slide back into the table beside the door, caused the lamp to crash to the floor.

She jumped when Liam and Murdock raced into the room. Liam's fisted hands were in a boxer's pose, prepared to tackle anything, the dog on guard.

"What happened?"

"It's frozen."

Liam stared down at the lamp. "Looks shattered to me."

"The computer, dammit," Hayley pointed a finger at the monitor. "It's frozen."

Liam walked over to brush a hand across the top of the monitor. "Feels warm to me. Don't see any icicles."

Hayley stared through narrowed eyes; didn't appreciate his jokes. "You idiot. I'm not in a joking mood. This is serious."

"Okay," he raised his hands, his eyes squinting as he studied her, "what happened?"

"I was copying and pasting between my notes file and the manuscript, then suddenly everything just froze. I can't do anything. The cursor won't move. None of the keys on the keyboard work. I can't save it. Close it. Nothing." She threw her hands up, walked away from him, then came back to glare at the computer.

Liam studied the laptop hooked up to the external drive hooked up to the monitor, the wireless keyboard and mouse on the pullout shelf. His heart skipped a beat when his eyes skimmed over the framed *Invincible like the diamond* note off to the side of the monitor.

"Can't you unplug it? Turn it off?"

"No. I don't want to unplug it; I might lose everything I did."

"You do backups, right?"

"Yes. And the computer automatically saves but that's not the point. What good are the backups if I can't access them on the *frozen* computer?"

Liam understood her frustration and how it affected her muse. He might not depend on the computer like she did, but he knew technology was a wonder when it worked; a bitch when it didn't.

He'd been battling his own set of frustrations. Every time he stared into her smoky green eyes, felt her toned body against his when they trained, sniffed her soft floral scent, or listened to her tears like he did last night. He'd slipped up yesterday in the heat of their argument and kissed her. Realized he wanted her but couldn't have her. Wouldn't let himself have her.

"Okay," he raised both hands, "you've been at it for four hours now. It's a nice day outside and you need to take a break. Walk away."

"I can't." She threw her arms up, paced across the room. "I have a deadline and I'm behind because I didn't get anything done yesterday. I just spent two hours on that scene and now it's gone."

She fisted her hands at the ceiling, wanted to throw her head back and scream.

Murdock pranced over, tried to lean against her but she turned, walked away.

"Screw the deadline," Liam unplugged the laptop from the external drive, tucked it under his arm and walked out the room.

"What?" Hayley jumped around. "What are you doing?" she exclaimed in shock. "Where are you going with my laptop?" She followed him into the hall, yelped when he tossed the laptop onto his bed, shut the door, and blocked her entrance.

"Give it a rest," he commanded out of the side of his mouth, arms across his chest. "The computer probably needs to catch up with you."

He pointed a finger at her. "You need to chill. Even if it started working right this moment, you're too frazzled to think."

He grasped her upper arms, turned her toward the stairs. "Go take a walk."

"I'm doing no such thing." She slipped out of his grasp, tried to sidestep past him to his bedroom. "I've had my jog for the day, I'm not in the mood for a walk. I have work to do."

"Not right now, you don't." Liam grabbed her hand, leaned down, tossed her over his shoulder.

"Put me down, you idiot."

"In a minute." He continued down the steps turned toward the front door where he deposited her on her feet on the front porch.

"Take a walk," he repeated before shutting the door in her face.

"Open that door," Hayley demanded, pounded on the wood frame when she heard the lock click.

"Take a walk," Liam shouted from the other side.

"I'll show you," she mumbled.

She charged down the steps, punched the code to the garage doors, leaned down to race inside as soon as they started up. Jogged between the vehicles in time to catch the click of the lock on the kitchen door from the inside.

"Open this damn door," she pounded the wood; kicked it, then turned, determined to try her last resort.

She heard the garage doors going down as she rounded the corner toward the back. Murdock greeted her jumping in excitement, followed her to the back deck where she found Liam sitting in one of the deck chairs, feet resting on the railing, crossed at the ankles.

She marched past him tried the sliding doors, found them locked.

"Open the door," she turned on him, her fisted hands on her hips. "Give me the key so I can open the damn door."

Liam stared across the yard, ignored her. He glimpsed the motion of her fisted hands and jumped up in time to avert her pounding blows. He snarled, decided he was getting tired of being her punching bag.

"Why do I have to put up with you," she aimed for his chin, followed it with her other hand when he dodged it.

"You're always telling me what to do," she raised her hand. "Always between me and where I want to go," she snapped when he cupped her fist, nudged it behind her back.

Liam grabbed her other fist, backed her to the railing.

"Red," he tightened his grip when she tried to wiggle away, "Calm down. You need a break."

He stared down at her. Their bodies close, faces inches apart, lips a whisper away, he clamored for control. Vowed he would not repeat yesterday's kisses.

Hayley's heart pounded as she glinted up at him. Her breath mingling with his, her breasts pressed against his hard chest. She worried he would kiss her senseless again.

"Let me go," she insisted.

He continued to study her. "Are you going to behave?"

"I'm not a child."

Liam glanced down, appreciated the cleavage displayed in the vee of her shirt.

"I'm well aware of that," he smiled, started to loosen his grip, tightened it when she almost growled, squirmed in anger.

"Hayley, I know how frustrated you are. Believe me, but you need to relax more. The least little thing seems to anger you. I know you don't want me here and I wouldn't be here if I didn't have to. But your father is worried. I'm worried. And after what happened yesterday, we need to be more cautious."

She released the breath she didn't realize she'd held, rested her forehead on his shoulder.

"I'm worried too," she agreed. "And I understand why you are here. That doesn't mean I have to like it."

"I've been here less than a week and you're already frazzled. You get worked up at the least little thing. I've tried to be accommodating, not bother you but you need to take care of yourself. Come on," he released her hands, rested an arm around her shoulders, steered her down the steps, "I want to show you something."

"What?"

He pulled her closer to his side. "Come with me and you'll find out."

He headed for the path on the edge of the woods. They had started clearing the path just after she moved into the house, and she continued to work on it whenever the mood struck, or weather cooperated.

"You've done a good job clearing," he complimented her. "Might be edging a little too close to the front of the property though. Don't want to make it easy for them to find you."

"Yeah, I realized that a couple months ago. That's why I stopped. This path is another of my *thinking* projects."

She paused when they came to a Y in the path. "What's this?"

"What I wanted to show you. You're not the only one to use the path as a relief for tension." He reached for her hand. "It's a little steep."

They hiked up an incline, walked a couple hundred yards before he stopped.

"Listen."

Hayley concentrated. Listened to the quiet, the birds, breeze in the tree branches high above their heads. Then she thought she caught the babble of water.

"Is that water?"

Liam nodded, led her to a small clearing at the base of the mountain where a small waterfall drifted over hard rock into a stream.

"I had no idea this was here," she exclaimed.

"I happened to hear it after the rain the other night. I think it's a tributary of the West River."

Hayley could tell where he had begun clearing the undergrowth, stacked brush and kindling in neat piles off to one side.

"Might be worth tracking," she suggested. "Find out where it starts. Where it ends."

"Oh, I know where it ends. Keeps meandering south. It's the Champlain Creek that parallels the main road."

"Humph. And to think I have the little waterfall here on my property," Hayley beamed.

"I started working on clearing it day before yesterday. Figured since the patio was pretty much finished, it could be another *thinking* project for you. Place to work off stress. Unwind." He handed her a pair of gloves from his back pocket. Put the second pair on.

"Maybe unravel frayed nerves while a certain computer thaws."

Liam jogged back to the house for the wheelbarrow and rakes.

"This could be another escape route," Hayley suggested as she raked small brush into a pile, leaned on the rake to appraise the clearing, felt a sense of accomplishment to see it was beginning to take shape. She turned toward Liam when he remained quiet. Found him watching her work with a smile on his face.

"My thoughts exactly," he answered her questioning look, appreciated her healthy pinkened cheeks. Glad to see her indomitable spirit was rejuvenated. "If you're ever in a situation, have enough warning and a head start, you could probably hike through the woods from here to the main road."

They worked for three hours. Clearing more of the area, stacking wood for the future fire pit, found big logs which they situated in an area for meditation. Sat for twenty minutes watching the water, listening to the quiet, smelling the pine, evergreen, freshness of the air.

She returned to the house, decided she needed to take the rest of the day off. Visit the Farmer's Market to finalize the patio project with some bright flowers for the bench.

"I'll go with you," Liam decided. "I need to stop by the hardware store, pick up the paint for the blocks."

Hayley started to object. She was sure word had circulated about Kyle's adventure here yesterday. Didn't want to give them more to talk about.

"I'm going," he countered. "I'll park on the outer edge of the parking lot, observe from afar if I have to, but I'm going."

Liam sat in the truck, waited while she strolled among the vendors, check out the flowers.

"Screw this," he mumbled after ten minutes. After the exercise at the waterfall, he needed to keep moving or he'd be stiff. He climbed out of the truck, wandered in the opposite direction but kept her within sight.

He was leaning against a tree, when he glanced over, spied Jack Collins approaching from across the parking lot.

The Sheriff nodded his head toward where Hayley visited with the vegetable vendor.

"You two not speaking today? Saw you arrive together but go your separate ways."

Liam gave the Sheriff a crooked smile as he stared across the way. "No, sir, just giving her some space."

Jack crossed his hands on his chest, shifted on the balls of his feet.

"You know, after our little incident yesterday, I decided to do a background check on Amelia Cox. Just to be sure her 'spot of trouble' as you called it wouldn't bring any more intruders."

Both men watched in silence as Hayley wandered the different booths.

Liam swallowed, clenched his jaw. Figured it was a matter of time before the Sheriff would come sniffing. Decided to let the Sheriff sniff a little harder.

"Funny thing," Jack studied Hayley, "I couldn't find anything on Amelia Cox before two years ago. It's like she just appeared out of thin air."

"Hmm." Liam answered, also watching Hayley. Wondered if she was experiencing the vibes of their scrutiny, if she would look their way.

"I decided to do a deed search on her property. Discovered it is owned by *Connecting Associates.* Any other time, I wouldn't be bothered, but I used to be a detective in New York and recognized the business. Am familiar with the owner – Gerard Turner. Met his wife at a police fundraiser before she was killed."

"Hmm," Liam repeated, continued to concentrate on Hayley.

Jack smiled to himself. "I moved here five years ago but still have my contacts in New York. Still keep up with the news. Recalled an incident where Gerard Turner's daughter – Hayley – was instrumental in bringing down William Ortiz. Then she disappeared."

Liam turned to the Sheriff. "Sir, I'm not denying anything you've said but my job is to protect that lady over there. She had her world turned upside down five years ago but through sheer hard-headedness, perseverance, and bravery, she rebounded and is making something of her life. I'm afraid her world's about to be turned upside down again and I am determined to make sure she stays safe."

"I understand son, and this might not be the place to discuss it, but I just wanted to share that I am more aware of the situation and just as determined to keep her safe."

Jack tipped his hat to Liam, cast one more look at Hayley. "You do your part, I'll do mine."

The Sheriff wandered in the opposite direction.

Liam stepped toward the back door. "I'm going to walk the premises, walk off some of the stiffness."

He'd been fidgety since their visit to town. His talk with the Sheriff.

They'd both worked on their projects – she planted her flowers, he'd painted the blocks, spread more sand between the pavers. They'd enjoyed dinner at the table on the deck, appreciating their hard work.

His conversation with Sheriff Collins bothered him. It should have been a relief that the local Sheriff was aware of Hayley's situation but acknowledging his determination to keep Hayley safe triggered his personal feelings. He recalled the way his heart began to race when he realized she was more to him than just a job. The more he was with her, the more he realized he wanted her.

Hayley paused from rinsing the plate. They'd worked side by side all day and she still hadn't thanked him for the way he comforted her last night. She'd been stewing all day on how to thank him.

"Liam," she turned from the sink, stopped him before he opened the door. "I need to thank you."

"Thank me? For what?"

"For today. Taking me to the waterfall. Finishing the patio. Last night." She hesitated when the frown creased his forehead. "After my dream. Liam, there could never be *just* you."

Liam stuffed his hands in his pockets, stared down at his feet.

"It's *you*," she continued. "You've been there when I needed you. Taken care of me. Kept me in touch with my father. Much as I hate it, you always know what buttons to push."

She reached for the towel, dried her hands. Stepped toward him.

He made her nervous as he watched her approach.

"You've been there..." she stepped closer until she was in front of him. She leaned closer, kissed his cheek.

"This past week has been so stressful; I know I've been difficult to live with. I've taken it out on you, and I apologize."

Liam continued to gaze at her, his eyes flip-flopping between her eyes and her mouth. He tilted his head to brush her lips with his. "Thank you."

While he still had control of his feelings, he turned, stepped toward the door but stopped.

"Just to let you know, at the rate we're going, it's a matter of time before we're in bed together. For more than comfort after your nightmares. Count on it."

Hayley swallowed hard when he opened the door, stepped outside. She returned to the sink and smiled.

Chapter Eight

Liam glared across the parking lot at the Farmer's Market, tapped his fingers on the steering wheel, wondered why he was there. Because you screwed up, he grumbled to himself. He'd been steamed with himself all morning for caving to his emotions – the volatile kisses the other day, soft one last night. Uptight and edgy that his feelings for Hayley were getting harder to control.

He'd needed to duck out of the house for a while. That light kiss unhinged him. Baffled him the way he had reacted so calmly. Kissed her so freely. Was he getting too comfortable around her.

Maybe he should have stayed away. Sent someone else. Too much close contact made him more aware of her body; his seemed to be in a constant state of unrest. He worried he wasn't as alert, agile as before and might not be as objective where her safety was concerned. He was getting too close.

He'd taken Murdock for an early morning jog hoping to clear his mind, work out the tension. But when he kept looking to the stairs, ordering himself to relax, pull it together, he decided he needed to abscond.

Fuck, he muttered as he rubbed the back of his neck. He bolted out of the truck, slammed the door and strolled across the parking lot. Hands in his pockets, he scowled down at the bright vegetables – green, red and yellow peppers, onions, tomatoes, eggplants, too many for him to eat – arranged on the table of the vegetable stand.

"Where's Miss Amelia?"

Liam looked up, stared into the wide-set sunny blue eyes of the tall, stout vendor studying him. He had a ruddy complexion that needed a shave, square face with wrinkle lines on each side of his mouth and receding hairline of almost white hair. Liam guessed him to be in his late sixties.

Liam cleared his throat. "Excuse me?" He mumbled out of the side of his mouth.

The man tapped his Roman nose. "You've been here before. The same time as her. The other day in fact."

Liam considered the gleam in the old man's eyes behind the wire-rimmed glasses and glowered.

"It's not like that. We're just friends," he responded with a clipped voice.

The man's mouth twitched. "Not my business. But seeing as you're all bent out of shape, she must be mad at you," he persisted. "That why she wouldn't shop with you the other day? Why she's not here this morning?"

"Actually, she's working." His jaw clenched; Liam responded through his teeth with forced restraint.

"I caught the way your eyes followed her." He smiled, shrugged a shoulder. "Guess if I had a woman like that, I'd watch her too."

"It's not like that," Liam repeated.

"None of my business." The old man shrugged a shoulder, turned to add tomatoes to his display.

"Look," Liam grimaced, "we're friends. Okay? She's had an upset from home and I'm just trying to help."

"None of my business," he repeated as he tossed the storage box under his table. "You going to buy anything or not?"

Liam reached for the tomatoes the man had just set out. Grabbed four ears of corn, decided despite his gruffness, he liked the man. "You seem to have a good perspective on the area. You lived here long?"

"All my seventy years."

"You set up here every day?"

The vendor nodded. "Gives me something to do, keep up with the gossip."

"Have you observed anyone new in the area?"

"Besides you?" His eyebrows arched above his glasses.

Liam's lips twitched. "Yeah, besides me."

The old man shrugged, looked left and right of his table. "No more than usual. You're the only one to stay."

Liam handed the old man one of his cards. "If you should see anyone suspicious, would you give me a call?"

"Suspicious, huh. You expecting trouble?"

Liam shrugged a shoulder.

The man studied the plain card. "Can't be too bad," he decided, "noticed you talking to the Sheriff the other day."

Liam handed the man a twenty, reached for the bag. "Like I said, I'm just a friend."

The old man held onto the bag when Liam turned to leave. "Take care of your friend." He added a carton of strawberries to the bag. "I like her too."

Liam was about to thank the man when his phone pinged an alert. After a quick scan, Liam waved goodbye to the vendor, raced to the truck.

"Go to the stairwell. NOW." He texted Hayley.

'Why?" She replied at once.

"Just do it, NOW. Keep an eye on the cameras."

Five minutes later, Liam pulled off the main road into the driveway, pleased to find the gates still secured. He'd seen no vehicles along the side of the road on his way into town, figured whoever was trespassing must have parked further up the road and hiked in.

His phone had sounded several more *motion detected* alerts as he drove. He pulled up the images, detected the perp dressed in camouflage, a rifle draped over his shoulder. Another alert pinged. Liam determined he was on the far side of the property working his way toward the back of the house.

Liam grabbed his Glock from under the seat, tucked it behind his back, sprinted through the woods. It appeared the perp had discovered the waterfall trail and was making his way to the back of the house. Liam hoped the perp wouldn't be expecting anyone to ambush him from behind.

Minutes later, Liam was within sight of where he suspected the intruder to be but found nothing. There were no sizeable bushes offering a hiding spot. Eyes squinting, Liam studied the area almost missed the tip of the silencer at the end of the rifle as the perp, lying flat on the ground twenty yards to his left, shifted the rifle off his shoulder, aimed it at the house, scoping the windows for interior movement.

Certain that Hayley had followed his orders and was safe in the stairwell, Liam squat behind two tall morphically joined oaks, decided to wait. See what the perp did. Figured he wouldn't sit still too long, not after the long hike onto the property. Probably wanted to sneak inside, get the job done, then move on.

Sure enough, the guy rose, made his way from tree to tree toward Liam, his eyes focused on the dining room side of the house that had the least windows. Liam waited until the perp was within ten yards before he charged from behind the trees, tackled the guy into the open back yard.

Hayley hated that Liam had interrupted her when she was in the middle of an intense scene between Faith and Kyle but didn't question his order. She'd motioned for Murdock to follow her, secured them within the stairwell and sat on the top step to study the wall of monitors for movement. Like Liam, she glimpsed the camera shots of the intruder making his way toward the house. Knew when Liam arrived at the front gate, began to track the intruder.

It amazed her all the planning Liam he had put into securing her house as she studied the fifteen camera views – eight for the inside of the house, seven outside. It had been twenty minutes since he'd texted, five since the last motion detected. She debated how long she should wait when she noted two figures come sprawling onto the ground at the edge of the woods off the back deck.

She jumped up, covered her mouth with a hand as Liam landed on top of the man whose forehead connected with the hard ground. She wanted to cheer when Liam jerked the strap of the rifle from the guy's shoulder, tossed it away from them then reach for his Glock and hit the man on the back of his head.

Still straddling the guy, Liam reach for his phone.

"Call nine-one-one and bring me some zip ties. Quick." he texted Hayley.

"You're going to need to stock up on those zip ties," Jack Collins joked with Liam when he and one of his deputies joined them in Hayley's back yard.

"This one seems to have suffered a little more," Jack eyed the goose eggs – one in the middle of the guy's forehead, another on the back of his head. Noted he was also sporting a bleeding fat lip.

"He was a little mouthier than the other one," Liam snarled. Recalled the perp's warning that more were coming.

"We'll give our FBI guys another call." Jack waited until the deputy left with his prisoner before he turned to Hayley.

"Ms. Turner, do you mind if we sit and have a little chat?"

Hayley blinked that Sheriff Collins addressed her with her real name. Cast a look at Liam who tilted his head to let her know it was okay.

"In that case, would you like to come inside for some coffee?"

"I had a little conversation with Mr. Walker the other day," Jack stirred creamer in his coffee, "told him I'd done some researching and couldn't find anything for Amelia Cox beyond two years ago. He wasn't too forthcoming but considering these recent trespassing incidents, I need to know a little more about your situation."

Hayley wrapped her fingers around her mug, to warm the cool chill that enveloped her body.

"In my digging, I discovered that Gerard Turner owns this property. I also learned that his daughter Hayley Turner was brutally attacked five years ago and assisted in the conviction of William Ortiz who is now serving a life sentence at Attica. How am I doing so far?"

Hayley nodded her head. "Sir, it's not a case of not trusting you"

"I'm not questioning that," Jack raised a hand to interrupt her. "I just need a little more information so I can better protect you."

"Sir," Hayley shifted in her seat, stared into her cup trying to decide how to best tell her story. "William Ortiz murdered my best friend, Judith Toliver. She and I grew up together, attended college together, shared an apartment after college. I went into modelling. Judith worked as an accountant for William Ortiz and was dating his nephew. She detected some discrepancies in the books and expressed her concerns to his nephew. Somehow, word must have gotten back to Ortiz because one night I came home to find Judith being beaten by this big, gruff, angry man. After he shot her, he realized I had come in the back door and was hiding in the kitchen. He decided to beat me. Thought he'd killed me as well."

Hayley took a deep breath as the memories came flooding back.

Liam reached for her hand.

"Hayley survived the attack but suffered amnesia for several weeks. When she regained her memory, she recalled Judith giving her a USB flash drive which turned out to be backups of Ortiz's books. From there, the feds froze his accounts and with Hayley's testimony William Ortiz was convicted of Judith Toliver's murder. They never caught the henchman."

"It didn't stop there," Hayley continued her story. "There was an attempt on my father's life, then on me. My father hired Liam to train me, protect me, and I've pretty much been in hiding, living under an assumed name ever since. Sir,"

Hayley cast eyes brimming with tears toward Jack Collins, "I haven't seen my father in five years. William Ortiz may be in prison, but he has made my life a living hell. And he may have had another friend murdered trying to find me."

Jack frowned, looked from Hayley to Liam.

"Savannah Hughes was murdered in New York last month," Liam explained. "Hayley writes under the pseudonym of Jillian McLeod and Savannah was her point of contact with the publishers. We think Ortiz somehow discovered that link and murdered Savannah trying to locate Hayley. Considering the two recent trespassing incidents, it's obvious the location of Hayley's safehouse has been compromised. That's why I am here."

Liam hesitated, gave Hayley's hand another squeeze.

"I also have reason to believe William Ortiz has issued a bounty on Hayley."

"**B**ounty? Seriously?" Hayley argued as soon as Sheriff Collins left.

"Why do you think the last guy had a busted lip?" Liam scowled at her. "Before you joined us outside, he told me more were coming."

Hayley's mouth fell open. "What good is it going to do to kill me? It'll only add to his sentence. Like he's going to be released in this lifetime. He's already lost everything. Why is he so determined to kill me?"

"Vengeance. Retaliation. To even the score. You took away his independence. Ended everything for him. Hayley, William Ortiz is a dangerous man. I haven't talked to your father yet, but we might need to rethink things."

"No," Hayley shouted. "There will be no more rethinking. I am not changing a thing. Not changing my location, my routine, what routine I have. Nothing. I refuse to let that jerk control my life again. Things were settling down. I have my writing. This house. I will not let him dictate my life. I'll just have to stop them one by one."

She stomped over to door to the basement, raced down the stairs.

Liam was certain she intended to take her frustration out on the punching bag in the gym.

He found her there thirty minutes later, stripped down to her sports bra and tights. Her body slick with sweat, shoulders squared, face flushed, she breathed hard as her pink hand wraps jabbed, crossed and hooked the bag.

"Red, you need to rest." He shook his head when she ignored him. Stepped over to grab her from behind, make her stop. Cool off.

He ducked when she turned at his approach, her eyes fierce as she took a swing at him. Fury overwhelmed him when he dodged the second blow. He didn't come down here to pick a fight. But she was out of control.

He could hear the exhaustion in her heavy breathing; her swings were like those of a spoiled, ill-tempered child. He dodged her next swing, worried his body was more attuned to her sweaty slick body, toned upper arms than dodging her swings.

She hooked a foot behind his knees and forcing him to fall backwards. She tried to straddle him but he overturned her, reversed their positions and pinned her beneath him. Trapped her legs with his legs, her arms above her head with his hand. Appreciated the feel of her breasts against his chest when she tried to buck him off.

Liam snarled when he realized he wanted to kiss her again.

"That's it," he beat the mat twice with his free hand, called the fight. "Hayley, you're exhausting yourself."

When she glared up at him, the air from her uneven breaths brushing across his face, he jumped up, turned to the stairs.

"You can't handle it?" Hayley shouted to his retreating back. Egged him on.

"Walking away?" she taunted when he continued toward the stairs.

Liam stopped in his tracks, fisted his hands. He understood her anger but damn if he was going to let her rile him. He would not let her push him to take it out on her.

"Oh, I can handle you Red. The problem is I don't think you can handle me. Or the feelings I have right now."

"Try me." Hayley jumped up, challenged him. "Or are you tapped out?"

Liam felt his blood boil. She knew better then to push him but maybe she needed to find out. He pivoted, his long legs carried him across the room as he delivered right and left-hand hooks interspersed with right and left leg kicks.

Hayley's eyes grew round, his unleashed momentum forced her to back away as she attempted to match his blows. Her heart jumped into overdrive as she found herself retreating, dodging hard, continuous punches and kicks. She twirled away from the wall, stumbled when he tripped her. Bit back a scream when he followed her to the mat, once again trapped her beneath his hard, angry body.

For one moment fear overwhelmed her as she stared into his hard eyes, witnessed the bottled-up fury before his mouth took hungry possession of hers. His tongue breached her lips, twined with hers as he angled his head, pressed her deeper into the mat while he struggled to control pent up emotions.

Liam tasted her fear, heard her muffled breaths as he assaulted her mouth. Released long repressed feelings that had been festering for days. When he felt her shiver, heard her soft murmur, he realized he'd gone too far.

He jumped up as if an explosive had discharged, flung him away from her. He stared down at her in disbelief, enraged with himself for losing control, taking the bait. Worried he could no longer protect her with an open mind.

"Maybe you're right," his chest rose and fell with rapid breaths. "Maybe you need a change." He turned once more for the steps. "I'll talk to your father. Have him send a replacement."

"No," Hayley shouted, breathing hard from the floor. Her mind might be frazzled from the last assault, but she was well aware she wanted only him protecting her.

"No," she repeated. "You can't leave. You're the only one who understands me. Stands up to me. You can't leave." She stared at his stiff back, her frazzled mind pleading for him not to leave.

"I'm sorry," she apologized. "I shouldn't have taken it out on you. Please," she begged, "please don't go."

Liam refused to look at her. He stepped toward the stairs, left her whipped and exhausted.

Later that evening, he listened for the tears.

She'd followed him up the stairs, showered then locked herself in her office. Liam was certain she murdered an army of characters. He realized it was useless to try to interrupt her, argue with her again so he'd waited for the tears. Lay in the dark of his bedroom, an anxious Murdock on the bed beside him.

When she'd come out at two in the morning, stumbled across the hall, Liam restrained the dog who wanted to comfort her. "Let her be."

An hour later, he heeded the tears, waited for the cry for help.

He threw the chair across the room as intense heat flushed his body. His pulse speeding, heartbeat pounding, he looked around for something else to fling but the room was bare.

Another foiled attempt. Another idiot had failed to get past Walker. What was it going to take?

After all these years looking, finally finding her, and no one could get her, he fumed.

What was it going to take to rid the world of the bitch that took down his empire.

He tightened a fist, imagined it connecting with her face.

More were coming, he bared his teeth. He'd seen to that.

She wouldn't have a minute's peace.

Chapter Nine

"Go pack a suitcase," Liam ordered the following morning. He'd been seated at the table, staring out the sliding back door for an hour waiting for her to awaken. Reliving the hellish events of yesterday.

He was agitated that the Ortiz situation was escalating. Debated the reliability of the perp's veiled threat; couldn't understand why it was so important to kill Hayley after all this time. Couldn't wait for the next perpetrator to breach their security and worried he might need reinforcements.

He'd been tempted to call his mother. She always had a way of centering him. Should have done it yesterday. She never snooped or criticized but listened while he solved, rationalized his problem. She would have reminded him he was named Liam for a reason. How she had named him seconds after he was born because of the first look they shared as mother and child.

"Your eyes were so dark, so direct, so determined. I thought of my uncle Liam who had been the strong one in our family. Took care of us after my father, his brother, was killed. When I gazed into your eyes, I was certain you carried the spirit of your great uncle."

Years later, after learning the meaning of his name – strong willed, protector, guardian – his mother had bragged how he was so brave as a child. Feared nothing. Always determined to be the best. How proud she was when he stood up for his friend who was being bullied in school.

He knew she worried about him when he served in Afghanistan. Continued to do so when he returned home, joined the Secret Service. Prayed for him during the darkest days of his life before he began working for Gerard Turner. Took on his most difficult, trying and frustrating job ever.

If he was going to protect Hayley, he needed to find answers.

He was annoyed his feelings for Hayley were becoming uncontrollable. Still angry about last night's fighting match in the basement; concerned he wouldn't be able to remain objective in his job. Realized it wasn't a matter of controlling his feelings for Hayley, it was a matter of how long before he took her to bed.

But he was more frustrated from lack of sleep. Those feelings might be simmering now but they would come to a boiling point if these nightmares and nightly comforting sessions continued. He wasn't a saint, could take only so many more nights holding her in his arms, comforting her.

Hayley almost jumped out of her skin when he'd yelled at her as soon as she rounded the corner from the stairs into the kitchen. She'd overslept, showered, decided to come down and get some of his coffee rather than make her own pot in her office.

"I told you I'm not moving." she tried to calm her racing heart, contain her shaking hand while pouring the hot liquid into her mug. It had not been an easy night, between their argument, the sparring match, fevered kisses, writing marathon, and nightmares.

She hated that the nightmares were becoming rampant. Recalled his coming to her bed, was thankful she was alone when she awoke.

So much had been said. She still wasn't certain he was staying. Or was he shipping her off to her father and his round the clock security?

"You're not moving. We're going on a little road trip."

She leaned against the kitchen counter, folded an arm around her stomach as she studied him over the rim of her cup.

Did he say *we*, she wondered.

"Road trip?" she gulped some hot coffee. "Where? How long?"

"Not sure. Just pack enough clothes for a couple days."

"Liam, I can't leave this house, go on a vacation. I have a deadline. And if an army of thugs is coming to kill me, what's to stop them from breaking in? Trashing the place? Waiting for us to return?"

He gave her that obnoxious stare. Was not in the mood to listen to her complaints.

"This house and property will be quite secure while we're gone. No one can break in here without my knowing about it. Wherever we are."

After his subconscious *chat* with his mother, he'd decided maybe they needed a change of scenery and made some calls. Pulled some strings, called in favors. Wasn't in the mood for another argument right now.

"Liam"

Her voice interrupted his thoughts, and he was certain by the tone of her voice she would continue to resist unless he maintained control.

"Do you want an adventure or not?" He rounded on her with a clipped voice. "Go pack your bag and be ready in forty-five minutes or I leave without you."

Hayley blinked, surprised with his gruffness. After the argument last night and his current mood, she didn't doubt he would leave her.

But she needed more information.

"Where are we going?" She persisted. "I need to know what to pack."

"For God's sake, Red," he threw his arms in the air, "just pack something to relax in, sleep in, go out to dinner. Weren't you a Girl Scout? Don't you know how to be prepared for anything? Can't you do what's asked for once? Do you always have to question everything?"

Considering his short fuse – for which she admitted she was probably responsible – Hayley tossed the liquid coffee down the drain, set her empty cup in the sink, headed for the stairs. Decided she'd play along.

Adventurous? She'd show him. She'd pack the whole damn closet, she fumed as she stomped up the steps to her bedroom.

She could be adventurous. Even if it was a chance to eat at a drive thru, sleep in a dingy motel room, watch a black and white TV, anyplace would be an adventure. Different. It had been two long years since she'd been more than ten miles from her home on the mountain.

She grabbed her backpack, crammed fresh underwear, sweats, the first available clothes that seemed suitable for travel. Dashed into her bathroom, grabbed her toothbrush and toothpaste, debated on the makeup. Was Liam worth the effort?

Hell, she decided, she'd do it for herself.

When she joined Liam in the garage forty minutes later, she discovered Murdock pacing nervously between their vehicles and felt guilty that she hadn't thought about the dog. If she was going out of town, she needed to find someone to keep him, feed him, spend time with him.

"What about Murdock?"

"He's going too," Liam opened the back passenger door to his truck, motioned to the dog to climb in. He reached for her backpack, opened the front passenger door, silently dispatched to her the same gesture.

Liam set the alarms, checked his apps, waited to be certain the entry gates locked behind him. After her objections about possible break-ins, he made a point of wrapping a heavy chain and padlock around the center railings where the two gates met.

Hayley remained silent when he returned to the truck, cast an indignant expression her way, then headed for the interstate.

Neither of them said a word for the first fifty miles. Liam was determined to cool his temper before arriving at their destination, Hayley refused to ask for more details. After two hours, she surmised they were headed for Boston, but knowing him, his current state of mind and paranoia, she wouldn't be surprised if he changed directions. She knew she wasn't in the mood to have her head bitten off again.

Five miles outside the city, Liam exited the interstate, turned into a shopping mall, parked beside a black Tahoe SUV with dark tinted windows.

"Wait here," he ordered as he cut the engine. Climbed out of the truck to shake hands and chest bump with a tall, muscular guy. He had ginger hair, a broad smile, bright teeth.

Hayley jumped when Murdock yipped with excitement from the back seat. When Liam opened the back door, the dog jumped out, his sleek body twisting in all directions from head to tail as he greeted the guy.

Liam opened Hayley's door, offered a hand to help her down.

"Brandon Anderson. Hayley Turner." Liam introduced them while transferring his and Hayley's backpacks to the SUV. "Brandon works for your father. He's going to drive us into the city, take care of Murdock while we're there."

"I don't think we've met, but it's pretty obvious Murdock knows you very well," Hayley shook hands with Brandon as she watched her dog jump into the crate in the back of the SUV.

Obvious affection glowed in Brandon's brown eyes as he brushed Murdock's short mahogany fur one last time before hooking the gate. "Yeah. Murdock and I go back to his puppy days. I helped Liam train him."

"With this spur of the moment plans, I don't trust anyone to board him," Liam explained. "Doubt that Murdock would either."

Brandon opened the back passenger door for Hayley.

"I'm in charge of your father's security team. He talks about you all the time."

Happiness bloomed inside her as Hayley climbed inside the vehicle. It cheered her to know her father spoke about her often. Missed her as much as she missed him.

Brandon might live in New York, but he drove the Boston area like he was at home – fast and aggressive. Ten minutes later, he turned into an underground garage, drove past several parked vehicles before stopping.

"This is where we start walking." Liam pulled a blonde wig out of the bag resting on the seat between them. "You need to put this on."

He placed a Red Sox baseball cap on his head, pulled it down over his eyes.

"What about our backpacks?" Hayley tucked her braid on top of her head.

"Brandon's taking care of that."

"But how will he know where we're staying?" She reached for the wig to cover her hair then fluffed the long champagne strands around her face and shoulders.

"Taken care of," Liam answered.

"But we haven't even checked in anywhere."

"Red, will you just shut up and trust me?" Liam pulled her out of the SUV, waved to Brandon who was shaking his head while laughing at Hayley's constant barrage of questions.

It was close to three in the afternoon when they stepped out of the parking garage, headed up the street. Since Liam was still out of sorts, Hayley decided to play along. Her mood had lightened considerably after Brandon's comment about her father, but she was also happy being in a new environment.

She took a deep breath, appreciated the different surroundings. It had been so long since she'd been on a busy street full of pedestrians. Everyone was in a hurry, talking or scrolling on their cell phones while they navigated the concrete sidewalks.

Unlike Champlain, Vermont which boasted one stoplight, there were traffic lights on every corner where cars, buses, limos and bikers fought to get to their destinations in record time.

She inhaled the scent of coffee as they passed a busy café, perfume that wafted from the open doors at the *Bloomingdale's* department store, onion and garlic from ritzy restaurants, exhaust fumes of vehicles.

She studied the tall buildings, street vendors, window displays, people seated outside restaurants enjoying a late lunch or early dinner. Felt the autumn breeze at the intersections; heard people talking on their cell phones, honking car horns, sirens in the distance and smiled.

It was all so wonderful. Extraordinary. Incredible. And she'd missed it.

Her eyes grew wide when she realized they were about to enter one of the most exclusive hotels in the city.

"Keep your head down," Liam murmured from the side of his mouth as they stepped through the sliding doors, "don't look at anyone."

He put his arm around her waist, pulled her close as if they were lovers and led her to the wall of elevators.

As instructed, Hayley kept her head down but peeked sidewards as they passed people waiting at the reception desk, valets loading luggage on shining gold carts, guests lounging in chairs around the big fireplace.

She continued to avoid eye contact when they stepped into the crowded elevator, turned her back to the glass wall that looked over the lobby. Resisted gazing down on the luxury as they were lifted to the twelfth floor.

"Brandon's already checked us in," Liam explained in answer to her surprised expression as they made their way down the wide hall. "Our backpacks will be delivered soon."

He scanned the key card over the magnetic key slot, moved aside for her to enter ahead of him.

Hayley stepped inside, appreciated the whitewashed brick walls, floor to ceiling windows with a balcony beyond. There was a mini kitchen on the right of the entrance, seating area with upholstered chairs, sofa, fireplace with flatscreen TV above the mantle. Paneled wood sliding barn doors on either side of the seating area led to the bedrooms.

She crossed the lush carpet toward the balcony, saw that the suite looked over the world-famous *Fenway Park* baseball diamond.

Thousands of seats on tiered levels surrounded the playing field. She recognized the retired numbers of some of the Hall of Famers – Carl Yastrzemski, number eight; Ted Williams, number nineteen, Wade Boggs, number twenty-six, Carlton Fisk, number twenty-seven, Jackie Robinson, number forty-two – showcased on the right field facade.

She assumed the Red Sox would be playing soon as she observed the crew preparing the field, stands beginning to fill with spectators.

Hayley took an excited breath. "Oh, Liam, this is amazing."

She turned at the sound of the barn door on her left sliding open and her whole face lit up. Her eyes widened in amazement and heart lurched to her throat when she found herself staring into her father's gray eyes.

"Daddy," she gasped, before running into his arms.

Liam nodded to Gerard Turner, backed into the hall, and headed downstairs to the bar.

Chapter Ten

"I can't believe you're here," Hayley sobbed into her father's chest, inhaled his familiar cologne and hugged him tighter.

Gerard Turner rested his cheek on the synthetic blonde hair and hung on to his most precious gift. It had been so long since he'd held his little girl in his arms. He chuckled at the feel of the coarse fibers against his face and leaned back to search her eyes.

"Let me first be sure this is my beautiful daughter under all this hair."

Hayley giggled, reached up to yank the wig off her head. "Brandon's contribution to this adventure."

Her eyes roamed his long narrow face, chiseled cheeks, roman nose and thin lips. He hadn't changed much, still clean shaven with trimmed silver-gray hair but with a few more worry lines across his forehead. She stared into his steel gray eyes and embraced him again.

They continued to hold onto each other, turned their heads toward the balcony when the national anthem blasted from the speakers surrounding the ball field.

Rather than sit on the balcony that overlooked the ballpark, they decided to listen to the game from inside the room. They could hear the excitement from the distance, watch replays on the TV above the mantle.

This family reunion was more important. Emotions were high between father and daughter who had five years to catch up on. They held hands, afraid the loss of contact would break the magic of the moment. Eyes that sought the other stayed misty.

The game was in its second inning with no score. Gerard stretched out his long legs, crossed his feet at the ankles. He'd shed his black pinstripe business jacket, loosened the bold stripe tie. Hayley had tucked her legs beneath her, brushed her free hand over the necklace that rested on her chest.

"Liam called me. Said he thought you needed a change of venue." He chuckled. "Added he was tired of hearing the two of us talk about how we missed each another, so he pulled some strings. I'm glad I was able to reschedule a couple meetings."

Gerard studied his little girl – she would always be his little girl – gave her another kiss on her forehead, elated to have her so close. She was still as beautiful as ever, but her face was thinner. He didn't like the haunted look of her soft olive eyes and cursed the man responsible for putting the hint of shadows beneath her lashes.

Hayley frowned, turned her head toward the ballpark in the distance. Pressed her lips together in a slight grimace, thought about how difficult she'd been with Liam. How despite her ugliness, he had arranged this reunion with her father.

"I'm afraid I've been a little hard on Liam these past few days."

"Seems you've always been a challenge for him," Gerard squeezed her hand and chuckled as he listed Liam's descriptions of her. "Argumentative. Uncontrollable. Thorn in his side. Between you and me, I think he has enjoyed the challenges."

Hayley remained silent. Knew her father spoke the truth. Sparks had ignited between them from the moment she'd awakened, spied him dozing in the chair in the corner of her hospital room. She'd been grieving, hurting, recovering, and angry her life had been turned upside down; wanted nothing to do with anyone. Wanted nothing to do the physical therapists that pushed her to strengthen her muscles much less the stranger who appeared out of the blue, followed her on her road to recovery then one day told her she needed to stop feeling sorry for herself. Informed her she needed to learn how to defend herself, make something of her life. She hadn't appreciated the insult then but in hindsight, realized it was the push she'd needed to get stronger. Move on with her life.

"Maybe this little rendezvous is long overdue," Gerard confessed, "I apologize for that. But things were so hectic in the beginning. With you recuperating in the hospital, keeping your survival of the attack a secret, the trial, then the assassination attempts."

"I'm beginning to wonder if it will ever end," Hayley sighed. "I thought it had." She turned back to her father; still couldn't believe he was sitting beside her as her eyes roamed his face. "Much as I missed you, everything seemed to be going along okay. Then Savannah" she pressed her fingers to her lips, paused as her voice broke. Tried to control it. "Then another friend was killed, and my world has been turned upside down again. Just when I was getting used to my successful career, being on my one, Liam is suddenly back in my life. Back in control."

Gerard studied his daughter, worried at the frustration in her voice. He had always worried about the animosity he detected between her and Liam. Half-way wondered if the man was in love with his daughter to put up with all he had.

Gerard decided his daughter needed to know a little more about the man who protected her.

"Hayley, do you remember Ortiz's botched attempt to kill me? After the trial?"

"How can I forget?" She shivered. "It scared me to death."

"That wasn't the first time Ortiz had tried."

Hayley straightened, frowned at her father. "What do you mean?"

Gerard turned toward her, gazed at their still joined palms as he trailed the tip of a finger across the top of her soft hand.

"You were still in the hospital the first time. I was supposed to attend a Board meeting, but something came up and I couldn't go." He looked up. "Do you remember Grace Walker?"

Hayley smiled, recalled the pretty blonde woman that was her father's Executive Assistant. She had beautiful blue eyes that reminded her of a crystal-clear sky and always talked about her handsome husband who was forever away on assignment.

"Yes. She was so friendly whenever I stopped by the office." Hayley sat up straight and beamed. "And I remember her little girl, Zoe. She was so spunky, full of life. I thought it was so neat of you to let Grace bring Zoe to work those few times she had babysitter problems. How are they? Zoe must be in school now."

Gerard's mouth flattened as memories of his Assistant flickered through his mind. Grace had been a godsend, kept him organized, focused after his wife Julia, Hayley's mother, had died.

"Grace was in that car. Instead of me."

He hesitated a moment when Hayley inhaled a deep breath, then continued.

"She'd been having a bad day. Her car was in the shop, the babysitter was sick, so I told her to bring Zoe to work, offered to have them driven home that evening after work."

"Grace was in the car?" Hayley sobbed. "Was she"

Gerard's face softened as he nodded his head, recalled getting the news of the explosion.

"She, Zoe and the driver were killed by a car bomb that was intended for me."

"Oh, Dad, I'm so sorry. Grace was so nice, and her little girl was a darling. I used to give Zoe suckers whenever I visited."

"Yes." Gerard sighed, "But there's more. Hayley, you didn't know him at the time, but Grace and Zoe were Liam's wife and daughter."

Hayley's eyes grew round. Her face paled and her heart felt like it sank to her stomach.

"Oh my God," her hand covered her chest. She leaned forward. "Oh my God," she repeated, covering her face with her hands, her elbows on her knees. "That's so awful. I had no idea."

"Liam was in the Secret Service at the time. I've often wondered if he hadn't been out of country on assignment and available to take them home, if Grace and Zoe might still be alive." Gerard rubbed his hands up and down his grieving daughter's back.

"Zoe and the driver died at the scene, but Grace lingered for two days. Liam was devastated of course. Felt guilty that he wasn't there. He was flown back to the states, stayed by her bedside until she died. You were recovering in the same hospital, and I met him when I visited Grace right before she passed. It was difficult for him; his guilt drove him to resign from the secret service. When I realized you were going to be okay but would need protection, I approached him about the job. That's how it came to be that he is working for me, protecting you."

"I remember Liam visiting me at the rehab center, watching me during my physical therapy. He never spoke to me, always kept tabs on me. I guess I just didn't like him staring at me all the time and we got off on the wrong foot." Hayley turned to her father. "He has never mentioned his family to me. And I'm sorry I've never asked. Never made the connection with the last names."

"Liam is very good at what he does but he's also a private man. Considering that Ortiz has forced his way into our lives once again, I wanted to ease the tension between you and Liam. You need to be able to trust and understand one another."

Liam viewed the game from the bar downstairs. It was a long narrow space, probably intended as a watering hole for those looking for brief rendezvous or shot before heading up to the room. The wooden bar extended the length of the room, liquor bottles lined the mirrored wall behind it. A row of small tables in front of the windows on the opposite side of the room offered a view of the busy street. Situated to the left of the hotel entrance it also gave a bird's eye view of everyone entering or exiting the establishment.

He knew Gerard Turner needed to be back in New York City for a fundraising event that evening. They were cutting it close but that was why he'd acted quickly. Anyone tracking Gerard Turner's busy workday wouldn't pay any attention to a missed Board meeting if he was at the very public fundraiser afterwards.

It wasn't unusual for his boss to jet from city to city and it worried him that the logbook would reflect his current location. No one should think twice if he decided to attend a Boston Red Sox game two hundred miles away. And by the time anyone learned he wasn't alone but with the daughter he hadn't seen or talked to in five years, he and Hayley would be long gone.

Liam watched Brandon stroll through the lobby with his and Hayley's bags stuffed inside expensive luggage.

Brandon tipped the bellman to deliver them to the suite then joined Liam in the bar.

"The reunion going okay?" Brandon inquired as they settled at a round table at the far end of the room.

Liam nodded his head. "So far. They don't have too much longer."

Brandon checked the time on his phone. "Yeah. He's going to be a few minutes late as it is." He chugged his beer. "Do you think there's any truth to this bounty nonsense?"

"No telling," Liam leaned back, blew out his cheeks. "We've had two attempts and the second perp was pretty cocky. Not sure whether Savannah Hughes said anything or if they hacked her computer. I haven't had any more camera alerts on the house since leaving this morning. The Sheriff did some checking, is now aware of the situation."

"How's Hayley holding up?"

Liam shook his head as he studied his beer. "It's tough. She's tough but I worry when things heat up. She had a bad spell last night. Another reason I decided to change things up."

"This impromptu get together might be the best thing for them both. I know the boss worries about her."

Brandon was head of Gerard Turner's security team, coordinated the security for his daily calendar. Monitored the surveillance equipment, oversaw the team of guards, inspected the home, office and vehicles.

He'd started working for Gerard Turner after Julia Turner was killed in the car crash. Brandon had never met Turner's wife but was one of the team of detectives who investigated the case. He had serious doubts about the evidence and voiced his opinion when it was ruled an accident. When he'd shared those thoughts with Gerard Turner, after the car bombing that killed Liam's wife and daughter, the businessman had hired him on the spot.

Liam studied his empty glass. "If things are going to heat up, the two of them need this contact to recharge. Hayley does. Might not know when the next chance will come." Liam looked up when everyone cheered as the Red Sox hit a home run.

"I can't figure why it has started up again. The asshole is in prison, his funds are frozen. Nothing has happened for two years, why commence now. Unless he's been looking for her all this time. And if so, how is he funding it. Making the contacts. I'm inclined to visit Attica just to find out. Have a little chat with the bastard."

"I don't want to alarm the boss but I'm planning to do a major sweep of his office to be sure it hasn't been infiltrated. If I don't find anything, I'll do another background check on the staff."

"Guess it wouldn't hurt," Liam agreed. "Do the front office first. Check this new Assistant he has. If he catches wind of It, you'll be able to explain it better."

They both stiffened when their phones chimed in unison.

"Driver's almost here," Brandon stated as he prepared to forward the text to Gerard Turner.

Both men left cash on the table to cover their tabs and tip.

Liam headed to the wall of elevators, Brandon to lounge in a chair, make certain Gerard Turner exited the hotel with no problems.

Out of habit, Liam's eyes scanned the lobby area, checked for any suspicious characters that might be casing the area.

The sheen of the black tone-on-tone floral pants on the mannequin in the window of the hotel's gift shop caught Liam's eye. He detoured inside. Was certain the pants would spotlight Hayley's long slim legs, the deep green sleeveless blouse with a billowed hem her eyes and toned arms.

He added a black shirt for himself and headed upstairs to the room.

He rubbed the back of his neck as he paced the room. What was taking so long? Why was it so quiet?

Had everyone disappeared? He'd had no news for over twenty-four hours.

How difficult could it be to exterminate the woman? She was a sitting duck, holed up in her hideaway. All they had to do was get inside, get the job done, he fumed.

What was the good of hiring them if they couldn't do their jobs. Maybe he'd have to follow up with his other source.

Chapter Eleven

Hayley snuggled into the fluffy white complimentary robe, studied the outfit spread on the bed.

Liam had returned to the suite in time to chat a few minutes with her father before he had to leave for the fundraiser. He'd handed her the bag as soon as her father left, said they had dinner reservations downstairs in an hour, then proceeded to one of the bedrooms with his separate bag.

She'd tried the slacks on, and it amazed her that Liam guessed the correct size to purchase. Well, on second thought, he'd trained her, tackled her enough, he could probably guess close. She imagined him holding the legging like slacks up, gauging her size. Or looking around for a salesclerk close to her size.

What surprised her more was that he went to the trouble. She hadn't been very cordial, chummy these past few days. It made her feel special. He'd done so much already.

She coated her body with her calming lavender scented lotion and dressed. Studied her reflection in the mirror. The dark green top was short, the hem ended a tad below the waistline. Her fingers adjusted the cowl neck, so it highlighted her necklace. She did a half turn, pleased with how the sleeveless top showed off her slender shoulders, toned arms; leggings her long slender legs. She was thankful she'd thrown her black flat shoes into the bag at the last minute.

She debated wearing the blonde wig, decided not to. She ran her hands through her hair, brushed her long curls over her shoulder. If she was meant to die tonight, she'd die in style with her own hair. She was tired of living in hiding, welcomed the independence.

Besides, this trip had been so sporadic, who knew she was here.

She figured Liam agreed with her thoughts about the hair as he never suggested she use the wig. In fact, she noted he seemed to be at a loss for words when she stepped out of her bedroom.

She was pleased with his transformation. He might be easy on the eye, but she hoped his black attire – black tailored fit dress shirt with button down collar, black belt, black twill pants, black shoes – didn't match his mood. She breathed a sigh of relief when he gave her a half smile as he opened the door for her.

It had been so long since she had mingled in a crowd, Hayley was hesitant, self-conscious when the elevator doors opened. Taken aback at the large number of people milling about the lobby, some talking loudly, others chatting among themselves, all seeming to pay her no mind.

Since she didn't experience any nagging itch between her shoulders, Hayley took a deep breath, restrained the anxiety, accepted Liam's silent support when he took her hand, led her toward the restaurant.

Back straight, her head held high, Hayley strolled through the large room as if she was walking down a model's catwalk. Made her way past linen draped tables, exchanged glances with those who looked up, savored the harmony of the soft murmurs, lively conversations, boisterous celebrations. Smiled at the maître d' as he seated them in a semi-circular booth tucked in a corner of the restaurant.

Happiness sparked inside her as she accepted the menu, studied the selections, tried to decide what she'd missed the most the past five years – salmon, scallops or lobster. Settled on the smoked sea scallops.

With that decision behind her, Hayley set the large bill of fare aside, leaned back to wait for the wine. She scanned the room, let her gaze settle on Liam who was still studying his menu.

She fiddled with her earring as she recalled her conversation with her father about Grace and Zoe Walker. Felt sad that Liam had lost them so tragically and never told her. Didn't know how to broach the subject.

She was also grateful to be away from her house, thankful to him for arranging it, and didn't want to spoil the evening.

"You never told me about your wife and daughter," she finally blurted out, inhaled a deep breath when she realized what she'd said.

Liam blinked, surprised that her father would share his backstory.

"Didn't think it was necessary," he studied the menu, ignored the brief pang of hurt in his heart. "Besides, it was too personal. We were busy with training, getting you healthy." He lowered the menu to give her a veiled look. "Didn't want you to feel sorry for me."

Hayley was prevented from responding when the waiter arrived with their wine, went through the process of displaying the label, unscrewing the cap as it was a

Sauvignon Blanc, offering Liam his sip for approval, then filling their glasses the acceptable seven ounces.

After ordering their meal, Liam no longer had the menu to hide behind. The comment about Grace and Zoe unsettled him. Dredged up old memories of the darkest time in his life. He'd brought Hayley here to relax, get away from the stress, not bog her down with his trauma.

His eyes scanned the room, noted the couples scattered as twosomes and foursomes throughout the dining area. Eyed a group of five women chat among themselves as they were escorted to a table midway across the room. Laugh out loud as they immediately ordered cocktails and a bottle of wine.

There was a gathering of twenty or more in a small alcove off to the side celebrating a fiftieth anniversary judging from the big five oh numbers and balloons on the walls and gold decorations on the tables.

"Liam," Hayley interrupted his perusal, "after my father told me about your wife and daughter, it occurred to me that you've never shared any of your personal life with me." She blinked when Liam looked heavenward, tapped his fingers on the table.

"What do you want to know? I served in Afghanistan, went into the Secret Service when I came home. I was attached to the White House; part of the travel team that scoped the areas before the President was due to leave for a trip."

"So, you were a sharpshooter?"

Liam reached for his wine, nodded his head.

"I met Grace, we fell in love, got married. Had a daughter. It was an odd marriage because I was always on the road. Didn't see them as much as I'd wanted. My world ended when they died. I realized how much I'd missed and quit the service. Realized it wasn't worth it."

"You had a beautiful wife and a darling little girl," Hayley paused when he gave her a surprised look. "Liam, Grace worked for my father, I was bound to meet them. I used to give Zoe suckers whenever I visited my father's office, and she was there."

"Hayley, that was a difficult time in my life. I was in a bad place. Except for my mother who lives across the country, I had no family to go home to. Your father needed me to protect you. I needed the job to survive. Better than the travelling I had to do before. The only way I could put it behind me was focus on your training."

"But"

Liam let out a harsh breath. "Red, we came here to relax. Not dwell on the past. My past. If that's what you want, we can leave right now."

"I don't want to argue with you. I only wanted to say I was shocked when my father told me. To say I am so sorry." She reached across the table to cover his hand with hers. "You've been so considerate, and I've been so difficult. I appreciate what you did for me this afternoon. I didn't know how much I missed my father until I saw him today, so, thank you."

Liam regretted his harsh words as guilt washed over him.

"I think my father wanted me to realize you've had more than your fair share of tragedy as well. He knows how hot-headed I can get and wants us to be friends."

Liam's heart tripped when it occurred to him, he was falling deeper and deeper in love with this woman.

Before he could respond, their meal was being served, and they decided to enjoy the quiet, settled into pleasant conversation.

He noticed Hayley glance from time to time toward the group of women enjoying a girls evening, laughing, talking, sharing jokes. He was sure she missed the female companionship women seemed to need. He'd also observed two of the women look their way, exchange smiles with Hayley.

"Should we have been more discreet?" Hayley asked as they wandered out of the restaurant after dinner. "This trip has been so impromptu, no one, Ortiz's thugs included could know I'm here. Right?"

A smile tugged his lips. "I'd say we have a few hours on them."

The muffled music from the hotel's night club drew Hayley's attention and she cast a longing look at the darkened glass doors as they strolled by.

Liam reached for her hand, tugged her toward the entrance. Loud music and pulsing strobe lights greeted them when they stepped inside. Tiny white lights outlined the tops of dark walls, large speakers were mounted at the corners. The long bar with liquor bottles lining the mirrored wall was to the right of the entrance, stage for the band on the left at the back of the room. Small round tables were scattered around the wooden dancefloor and throughout the room. Waiters circulated carrying trays of drinks and shooters.

Liam searched the darkened room, spied an empty table on the far side of the dancefloor next to the women from the restaurant. He ordered wine for Hayley, two fingers of *Long Branch* for himself. Hayley settled back in her seat to observe. It had been so long since she'd been in a nightclub.

The band was excellent, two lead vocalists entertaining, songs inviting and energizing. It wasn't long before Hayley found herself bouncing to the beat in her seat, chuckling at some of the dancing moves.

The women from the restaurant were obviously feeling the effects of the alcohol which had loosened their party spirits as they gathered on the dancefloor near their table, bumping hips and moving to the beat, laughing at each other.

Liam's lips twitched when one of the women motioned for Hayley to join them.

Hayley's surprised eyes grew round. She looked at Liam as if asking for permission. She wanted to join them, enjoy the beat but didn't want to draw attention to herself either. She blinked when he gave her a broad smile, tilted his head, encouraged her to join them.

Liam appreciated the transformation as she laughed out loud, jumped up to join them, her arms and legs moving to the beat.

The band shifted and a staccato beat introduced the next song. All the women, Hayley included, threw their arms in the air and started laughing, squealing, bouncing to the fast beat.

"Shut up and dance with me," they sang the chorus with the band, their arms flailing in the air, hips gyrating, bodies bouncing, feet capering to the beat.

Liam saw Hayley brushing her hair into the air as she took pleasure in the lively acoustics.

It was an infectious song, Liam found himself tapping his foot to the beat. He saw one of the women exchange looks with Hayley, then look at him. Before he knew it, Hayley and the woman gyrated toward him, timed their motions to coincide with the next *shut up and dance with me* while pointing at him. He leaned back, shaking his head, but each grabbed a hand, pulled him onto the dance floor.

It had been a long time since he'd danced – not since Grace – but he quickly found himself dancing in place surrounded by the women, enjoying his moves while they rollicked to the infectious lyrics around him.

Caught up in the music, Hayley encouraged Liam as she frolicked around him, bumping against his hip, her hands brushing his shoulders, down his back, shouting *shut up and dance with me* with the band. She pointed her index and middle fingers between her eyes and him as if telling him to keep his eyes on her as they were *bound to get together, bound to get together*.

Liam appreciated that the song enlivened the crowd, but it also made him leery when he realized they had the attention of many in the room. Much as he didn't like being so conspicuous with all the women dancing around him, he decided what the hell, he was having a good time.

By the time the song ended, everyone was laughing, fanning themselves from after their active moves. Several in the celebrating group of women lifted their long hair from hot shoulders, hips sashaying as they made their way back to their table.

"And now," the lead singer announced, "we thought we'd slow it down a little with an *Unchained Melody*."

Liam snaked a hand around Hayley's back as the lead singer began singing.

"You got me out here" he called out, his eyes full of determination and desire. His hand settled at the small of her back, pulled her closer, "now it's my turn."

Hayley didn't resist. She grinned as she leaned into him, rested her head on his shoulder. Fell into his slow, unhurried stride.

She beamed when she looked over Liam's shoulder, saw one of the women sending her a thumbs up.

"Thank you for a wonderful day," she whispered into his ear.

Liam hugged her closer, his cheek against hers. "Let's enjoy the moment while we have it."

Hayley was familiar with the words – *Wait for me…hungered for your touch a long, lonely time…I need your love* - but hearing them sung by the tenor's soft voice, they meant so much more as they moved to the dreamy, easy song.

She'd hungered for a man's touch during her long, lonely isolation; appreciated the way Liam's hand leisurely brushed up and down her back. She sighed, followed his sleepy stride realized his love was all she needed. Hoped he would wait for her, stay in her life, put an end to all the heartache Ortiz was determined she live with.

Liam's desire flickered to life as he moved in lazy, sleepy strides, listened to the heartfelt words, inhaled Hayley's perfume and his arms cradled her against him. Heat coursed through his veins, and he realized he wanted, needed to show her his love.

As the song wound down for the final stains, he gave her a brief hug.

"We need to go," he murmured into her ear.

Hayley nodded in agreement, followed his lead as he made his way through the couples waiting for the next song. She turned back to the group of women to wave goodbye and was jostled away from Liam when rough hands wrapped around her waist, pulled her close.

"Come on baby, my turn to dance. Oof."

"I don't think so," Hayley announced as her knee connected with his crotch.

Liam turned in time to see her slam the jerk. He gave her a broad smile, approved her defending herself and reached for her hand to guide through the crowd.

They stepped out of the club, headed for the stairwell in the corner.

"I'm not climbing twelve flights of steps," Hayley tugged on his hand.

"We're not," Liam answered, "only two."

"But"

"Less crowded, less cameras this way."

"But"

"Hayley, trust me. As extra precautions, we're staying in a different room. Keep your head down, heed the cameras that are everywhere."

When he opened the door to the stairwell Hayley noticed there were steps that went down; read the *Parking* sign on the wall with an arrow pointing down to the underground parking garage. He led her up the flight of steps and before she knew it, he was opening another door, leading her down a long narrow hall.

Liam stopped three doors down, reached in his pocket for the key card as a group of four men stepped out of a room further up the hall and headed their way.

"Pretend to kiss me," Liam mumbled as he turned his back to the men, pulled her closer to his side.

"Why pretend?" Hayley stood between him and the door, wrapped her arms around his middle, began kissing the curve of his chin, her lips moved to his mouth while her hands ran down his back, to squeeze his butt.

She was so spontaneous, and enthusiastic, it caught Liam by surprise. He fumbled with the key card, almost dropped it. While her mouth assaulted his, he propelled her against the door that refused to open the first try. He managed to catch the knob at the green light on the second try, when Hayley's lips connected with his again.

He lifted her and stumbled into the room, slammed the door behind him. Listened to the cheers of the men as they walked past the room.

His arms still around her, her feet dangling between his, Liam tossed the key card across the room, pivoted to press Hayley against the door. Her head tapped against the hard door as his mouth captured hers, his tongue darting out to lick her lips, explore beyond.

Liam moaned appreciated the tight grip of those long tone on tone covered legs that wrapped around his waist. Impatient to be inside her, he cupped her bottom as his tongue took one more dip inside her mouth. With quickened breath, he turned from the door and stumbled toward the first bed.

He collapsed on top of her, pressed her into the soft mattress. His fingers aching to touch her everywhere, he began tugging at the hem of the blouse, nudged it up and over her head while she worked the buttons of his shirt, parted it to brush her hands up his smooth muscled chest.

He stood, gripped the waist of her leggings, and tugged them down and off her hot body. While he removed his own clothes, he studied the diamond necklace that rested between her luscious breasts, the stones glowing in the light from the bathroom.

Hayley's eyes followed his hands as he undressed, felt her nipples crest into hardened peaks as his eyes admired her breasts. She reached for him when he returned to the bed, held her breath, arched beneath him when his mouth latched onto her breast.

She parted her legs, offered her hot feminine core to accept his initial thrust.

It had been so long, they both took in a deep breath of surprise. Each paused to appreciate being filled, being surrounded.

“Wait for me,” Liam murmured into her ear, the words from the melody still flickering through his head as he felt her sweet warmth clamped around his iron hard length, accept him as he hammered her, built up the momentum as they chased after the passion that had been simmering since the moment they set eyes on one another.

Hayley felt a pang in her heart, her knees loosened as she experienced a shiver of delight and contentment thrill through her body.

Liam rolled off her, lay beside her on the bed. Waited for their bodies to cool down, hearts to calm.

Hayley had never felt so weightless, so drunk on happiness. She thought of the men in the hall and giggled. Felt her cheeks pinken when Liam looked over at her.

"Sorry," she turned on her side to face him, let her fingers dance across his bare chest. "I was thinking of those guys in the hall. Cheering you on."

The corner of his mouth curled up as he turned to face her. Brushed her hair over her shoulder, admired her exposed breast.

"You caught me off guard with your enthusiasm. It was all I could do to get the door open."

Hayley laughed. "They might remember us but don't think they'll be able to recognize us in a line-up."

Liam brushed the tip of his finger up and down her arm, causing her body shiver, nipple stiffen with desire.

"Are you looking for another round?" She challenged.

"Oh, I want more," he reached for her hand, tugged her off the bed. "First in the shower, then slow and easy in the bed."

They both fell into a deep sated sleep until Liam's cell phone awakened them at four in the morning.

Chapter Twelve

"We've got company." Brandon's clipped voice announced. "Got word two suspects entered the front lobby five minutes ago. Probably headed for the suite. Smart move changing the rooms. I'm approaching the parking garage. ETA two minutes. Will wait near the designated exit door."

Hayley looked over to see her clothes laid out on the other bed.

"You believe in being prepared," she commented as they dressed.

"Old habits."

They stuffed their evening clothes in their backpacks, threw them over their shoulders. Liam checked his Glock, tucked it in his jeans at the small of his back under his shirt and handed her a *Red Sox* baseball cap before heading for the door.

Hayley twirled her hair into the hat while Liam opened the door, checked the hall, found it empty.

With catlike speed, the moved past the doors to the two rooms between them and the exit, raced down the stairs toward the parking garage.

"When we go out to the SUV, I'll open the back door, you dive in. I'll jump in front. Stay low until we're out of the building. They apparently have someone watching the front of the hotel."

Liam eyeballed the switch on the wall beside the exit door; nudged it down to put the stairwell and their corner of the garage in darkness. He opened the door, sprinted over to the SUV, opened both passenger doors.

Hayley jumped inside, heard Murdock's greeting yip, reached over the seat to pet him, encouraged him to lay quiet.

Brandon navigated the vehicle around the interior row of cars, followed the exit signs painted on the pavement out of the parking garage.

Liam kept his hat pulled low, canvased for anything out of the ordinary. There was little traffic at this early hour, but he detected shadows in a vehicle parked on the street within sight of the hotel. They kept a close watch for any vehicles following as they maneuvered past the hotel, toward the interstate.

"You're sure they were Ortiz's men?"

"Positive. Two came in around midnight. Asked questions at the front desk. Sat in different corners of the lobby. Then two more came in thirty minutes ago. They had a little chitchat before those two went to the elevators. Guess they've discovered the suite is empty by now."

"How did they find out we were here?" Hayley inquired. She reached back to brush Murdock's head through the bars of his crate while Liam and Brandon exchanged silent looks.

"I want to know how the old man is funding all this," Liam grumbled.

"He hasn't had many visitors," Brandon commented. "I checked the prison logs after the Hughes murder."

Brandon pulled up beside Liam's truck still parked where they'd left it. "It's clean but considering they've discovered you're here; it doesn't hurt to check it again."

After verifying his truck was free of tracking devices and bombs, Liam okayed Hayley and Murdock switching vehicles.

"Take care of my father," Hayley called out to Brandon before shutting her door. After quick goodbyes, everyone was on their way.

Hayley leaned her head back on the seat, waited for her body to stop shaking, her heart to stop racing. After a night of dancing and lovemaking, followed by a few hours' sleep then their abrupt awakening, she doubted it would calm anytime soon.

She looked over at Liam, smiled as she studied his profile in the glow of the dash. The evening might have been cut short, but she had the memories of seeing her father, the fun on the dance floor, passion of being in his arms.

"I'm sorry," Liam interrupted her thoughts.

"Sorry? For what?" Was he regretting making love to her? She might be confused by the turn of events, but she wasn't sorry. Good sex was good for the soul. As far as she was concerned, it had been a long time coming.

"Seeing you with that group of women last night made me realize how lonely your life must be. No friends. Being by yourself all the time. When he offered me the job, your father shared with me some of your life before Judith Toliver's murder. Being a model. Do you miss it?"

Hayley breathed a huge sigh of relief to realize his mind was on a different track.

"Yes, I miss the hectic life. Sometimes. I enjoy the peace and quiet as well. Unfortunately, being my friend can be risky. Death for them. Too many questions for me. Besides wondering if I can trust them." She leaned back to pet Murdock. "Murdock's the only faithful friend I have, thanks to you."

Hayley reflected on how her life changed after Judith's murder. Yes, she was lonely which is why she poured herself into her writing.

"My characters are my friends. I enjoy creating them, giving them a story. They talk to me. There are a few people in town I enjoy visiting. Gladys at the grocery store who is always teasing me about my diet. James Fitzhugh at the hardware store who helped me with my patio project. Kyle the UPS guy, see what happened to him?"

She thought about Liam's threat to leave, find a replacement. The reason for their trip into the city. She didn't want to let on how much she had come to depend on him but felt he needed to understand how it upset her.

"You scared me the other night when you threatened to leave."

Liam jerked his head toward her, spotted the glow of bright tears glistening in her eyes. He reached for her hand, squeezed it.

"Red, I will never leave you. Not while Ortiz, or whoever, is threatening your life. Those words were spoken in the heat of the moment. We'd both reached our breaking point and spoke in haste."

Hayley breathed another sigh of relief. Sex might complicate things – was where they'd been heading since the day they met – but she could handle that. She was accustomed to being independent, taking care of herself. But now that things were heating up again, she was thankful that he would stand by her until the end.

"I don't understand how the jerk is keeping up with me," Hayley wondered out loud. "How could he have sent his goons so quickly? I mean, the trip to Boston was so impromptu. Right?"

Liam nodded his head. He'd been wondering the same thing but didn't want to upset her.

"Could it have been the dancing? Do you suppose someone saw us? Recognized me?"

"I doubt it, but we can't rule it out. My gut tells me your father may have a mole in his office. When we get back, I'm going to have Brandon check any recent hires. Someone in the office may have noticed his side trip to Boston."

"Has anyone attempted to breach my house?"

"No. But that might change now that we're heading back."

Hayley turned to look at him. "Thank you. For what you did. I needed that visit with my father."

"You're welcome."

"I didn't realize how much I missed my father until he was standing in front of me in that suite." She turned her head back to the front dash, gazed into the darkness ahead of them. "I hope it hasn't put us all in jeopardy again."

"Definitely proves we have somebody watching. We're going to have to be more careful from here on out. More observant. Don't take anything for granted and always be ready for the unexpected. But for now, you can continue your writing, I'll start digging deeper."

The sun greeted them when they arrived at the house. Since she was too exhausted to put one foot in front of the other, Hayley decided she was going to take a short nap before tackling her manuscript again.

Liam was too keyed up, had too many unanswered questions to relax. After making the call to Brandon to request a review of any new hires to Gerard Turner's staff, he decided to walk the property.

Brandon called within thirty minutes.

"The last new hire was Mr. Turner's new Executive Assistant. Five years ago." Brandon didn't want to mention Grace Walker's name, figured he could figure that out without dredging up bad memories. "She's in her early fifties, clean record so far. Only hitch is she's recently widowed. Husband was killed in a freak hunting accident."

"Hunting accident?" Liam wondered.

"Yeah. Went deer hunting last December. Didn't come home. She reported him missing and they found his body a week later. He'd been shot. Went by himself so they haven't determined if someone shot him by mistake. Hasn't been ruled a suicide but not closed either. I'll do a little more digging."

"Keep me posted," Liam ordered.

Before he could tuck his phone in his pocket it chimed again. He didn't recognize the number but answered anyway.

"You said to give you a call if I noticed anyone suspicious." Liam recognized Leo Murphy's voice.

"Yeah."

"Not sure if he's suspicious, I just don't like his looks. Got his license plate. You want it?"

Liam pat his chest, pockets, knew he didn't have paper or pen available. "Text it to me, I'm in the woods. Is he still there?"

"Yeah. Been here about thirty minutes. Sat in his car for a while. Then started making the rounds. Being Mr. Friendly. All smiles, good humor but I don't like him."

"He talked to you?"

"Not yet."

"I'm on my way."

Liam checked his messages, recognized the New York license plates. Called Brandon.

"Need you to run some plates. The car's been parked at the Farmer's Market for about thirty minutes. I'm on my way to check him out."

He sprinted back to the house found Hayley still sleeping and left a note.

Brandon called back while Liam was on his way to town to say the car had been reported stolen two days ago.

Since the Farmer's Market was located on the outskirts of the town, Liam decided to park on the Main Street, hike down to the open market. He followed a mother pushing a stroller with another child in tow as if he were the lagging father, scoped the area for anyone out of the ordinary. Spotted the newcomer right away with his leather jacket, designer jeans. Figured if he was fishing for information, he should have made more of an effort to blend with the crowd.

Liam exchanged glances with Leo Murphy, as the guy wandered up to Leo's booth and started making conversation.

Liam had also given the Sheriff a heads up about the stolen car and smiled when he saw the police cruiser pull into the parking lot.

Liam studied Leo's display from the far side as Sheriff Collins approached from the opposite side. Watched the man stiffen when he saw the officer.

"Hey, Sheriff. You looking for something for your pretty wife to fix for dinner?" Leo greeted Jack.

"I was wondering about that Buick over there. Have any idea who it might belong to?"

Leo nodded his head toward the new man. "I think I saw this guy drive up in it. That right?" he looked the guy in the eye.

"No, I think you must be mistaken," the man turned to leave.

Liam stepped over, stuck his foot behind the guy, made him trip and fall backwards.

"Mind if I check your license, fella?" Jack offered the man a hand.

"I haven't done anything," he brushed the seat of his jeans. "You don't need to be checking my license."

Leo decided to liven things up a little. "If you ask me, Sheriff, this guy's been acting a little strange. I observed him hassling Ms. Adams over there."

"I wasn't hassling anybody," the guy defended himself.

"Then what's with all the questions?" Leo leaned forward, his hands on his hips. "Don't even see where you've bought anything."

"I don't have to put up with this." The man turned to leave. He didn't move far before the Sheriff grabbed a hand and cuffed him.

"I think we'll continue this conversation in my office." Jack nodded his head to Liam, escorted the guy to his cruiser.

"Thanks for the tip," Liam shook hands with Leo. "I'll let you know what we find out," he added as he turned to walk back toward town.

Liam arrived at the Sheriff's office as Jack Collins was escorting his prisoner inside. The three men proceeded to Jack's inner office, closed the door.

"You know," Jack sat in the chair behind his desk, rested his elbows on the desk, crossed his arms in front of him. "I received a tip on a certain strange car that was parked at the Farmer's Market. Decided to run a check on it and discovered it was stolen." Jack leaned back, studied the man. "You know anything about that?"

"No, sir. Not my car."

"So, when my deputy comes back after doing a fingerprint check, he'll tell me he didn't find any of yours in the vehicle."

Jack noted the bobbing of the man's Adams's apple, overheard the loud swallow.

Jack Collins was a patient man. Had to be raising two teenage stepsons that were always getting into trouble. They always messed up. "We'll wait and see, then." He exchanged looks with Liam.

"Leo was saying you were full of questions for all the vendors. Are you looking for someone?"

Sweat beaded on the guy's forehead. "No, just passing through." He shrugged a shoulder. "Making conversation."

"In a stolen car?" Liam asked.

"I said it's not my car. What's with all the questions? And who are you?" The guy gave Liam a disgusted look.

"Concerned citizen." Liam answered.

"Maybe you can tell us which car is yours so we can make sure no one bothers it," Jack suggested.

"I locked it."

The Sheriff held out a hand. "Hand over the keys."

The guy pat his jacket pocket. "I must have left them in the car."

Jack Collins stood. “I tell you what, we’ll let you spend a little time in one of our cells while we unravel this mystery.”

Jack reached for the guy’s arm, but he jumped up, shrugged his arm away.

“Okay, Okay. It’s not my car.” He turned cold eyes on Liam. “You better get your affairs in order, buddy. Your days are numbered. More are coming.”

“The big guys and I are getting to be good friends,” Jack Collins joked thirty minutes later after the prisoner was escorted away. "How many more can I expect?”

Liam shrugged a shoulder, shook his head. “We were in Boston yesterday where she visited with her father and had four try to nab us there. I’m looking for answers. All I can ask is for you to be on alert.” Liam checked the time on his phone. “I really need to get back. We got in early this morning. She was sleeping when I left.”

Hayley was in the kitchen waiting for him when he arrived. She’d awakened an hour earlier, found his note on the kitchen counter, observed his arrival at the front gate and parking in the garage via the cameras.

“Problems?”

“Another visitor.”

She dropped the plate she’d been loading into the dishwasher. “Here? While I was sleeping?”

“No. Leo Murphy, your vendor friend called to say there was a strange guy at the market this morning. Texted me the license plate. Turned out, the car was stolen. Sheriff Collins came, we took him in for questioning and he finally confessed he’d stolen the car. He was also here for a purpose, said more were coming.”

Hayley collapsed on the stool at the bar. She was quiet as she fingered her necklace.

"I'm not leaving."

"I didn't say you were. I've got Brandon looking for answers; somebody is funding this and I intend to find out who." He stepped behind her, massaged her shoulders. "I want you to proceed as if nothing was wrong and let me find some answers."

She was quiet that evening. They were both exhausted from lack of sleep.

Liam knew she was putting off going to bed, worried the dreams would return so he gave her the space to work in her office, waited for her to retire for the evening.

He lay in his bed, listened to her tossing and turning in her bed. Much as he wanted her, he was determined not to go to her bed. It had to be her decision. He wasn't going to push himself on her. Take advantage.

Moments later, he glimpsed her shadow standing outside his door in the hall. He pulled back his covers, invited her to join him.

Missed them by minutes, he bristled.

After he'd been lucky enough to discover they were in Boston, and the goons still couldn't get them. Broke into the suite, found it empty.

Now the hotel was investigating, checking security cameras, questioning possible leads. All he needed was for one of the goons to be recognized.

Rage flashed through him. What would it take to get rid of her? Get the job done?

Chapter Thirteen

Hayley turned in the bed, snuggled beneath the covers and caught a whiff of Liam's scent on her pillow. She sat upright. What was Liam doing in her bed?

She glanced over to find his shirt draped on the chair beside the window. Realized Liam hadn't been in her bed, she was in his. Alone.

Then she smiled, covered her lips with her fingers. Recalled tossing and turning in her own bed, scared the nightmares would return. She hadn't wanted to be alone, so she ventured into his room, snuggled next to him under his covers and fell into a deep sleep.

She felt her cheeks pinken when she relived waking in his arms during the early morning. Recalled feeling his body jolt in awareness, hearing the slow, steady beat of his heart quicken when she snuggled closer, brushed her hand up to his shoulders, caressed the side of his neck, then his hair.

Her mouth curved into a smile when she recalled how he had lay still, while her fingers threaded through his hair, skimmed the beard along his chin, moved to his lips which opened, and his teeth nipped the finger.

Hayley stretched her arms above her head and fell back on the pillow as she recalled how he'd explored her body with his mouth. Her face, down her neck, his tongue circled the aroused bud of her nipple before returning to her mouth as he slipped inside her.

Where their first time together had been hurried and rough, this morning he had been slow, tender, gentle and affectionate.

She frowned, worried she could enjoy being in his bed on a regular basis. They weren't supposed to like each other.

She looked over at the clock and yelped. Ten o'clock. What was wrong with her, she scolded herself. She needed to get back to her writing. Meet her mental deadline. It had been three long days since she'd written a sentence, much less a scene.

She dashed into the shower, raced downstairs to see about breakfast. A good night's sleep, enjoyable sex, had whetted her appetite. Maybe a good night of lovemaking and full stomach would whittle away at the word count. Put some spice in Faith and Kyle's relationship.

Hayley stepped into the kitchen and jumped, surprised to find Liam seated at the desk in the corner of the dining area, studying the cameras.

"What's wrong?"

"One of the camera's is down," he mumbled out of the side of his mouth.

Hayley poured her coffee, stepped over to stand behind him, examine the multiple square visuals of the woods. One of the squares was black.

"My cell phone alerted me about thirty minutes ago. Could be someone is out there, or the camera is having battery issues. Been watching to see if any of the others pick up anything but so far, nothing."

At that moment another square went black.

Liam jumped up, grabbed his Glock. "Take Murdock, go to the stairwell and wait."

"Why not take Murdock with you."

"Not this time. Not till I know how many are out there. You watch the monitors in the stairwell. Do what you must do."

"Liam," Hayley called out to him when he stepped toward the door. "Be careful," she advised when he turned to look at her.

"You too." Liam nodded before sliding the door open.

"Come on, boy," Hayley called out to Murdock as she raced up the stairs to her bedroom and the secret chamber. Once again, they settled on the steps, studied the monitors. Like the computer screen downstairs in the kitchen, two of the monitors were black.

Within seconds, another went black.

Liam also saw the third screen go black as he studied the app on his phone. Based on the location of the downed cameras, he determined the culprit was working his way in from the front of the property. And armed with a screening device. Taking the cameras down as he approached the house.

He listened; thought he caught the sound of twigs snapping up ahead. He squatted down, searched the area, spotted the brown camouflaged figure slinking through the woods on his left.

He could have stepped out, ordered him to halt but he wasn't certain how many others there might be. He tucked the Glock in the small of his back, decided to let him come a little closer before ambushing him.

Hayley watched the camouflaged man approach another of the cameras. Without warning, he was tackled from the left, and she glimpsed Liam land on top of the guy. There was a scuffle, punches were thrown but Liam seemed to have the upper hand having caught the guy off guard.

She detected more movement from the porch camera aimed at the front drive. Another guy dressed in camouflage stepped away from the edge of the woods. She wondered if he could hear Liam and the other guy in the woods because he advanced in haste towards the front door.

Soon, he was out of sight of the camera but when she ran into the hall and listened from the top of the stairs, she knew he was working on the lock of the front door. Would be inside the house within minutes.

Deciding she needed a distraction, Hayley dashed into her office and pulled up a recorded interview she had done for one of her books. She turned up the volume, so it sounded like she was in the room talking to someone on the phone.

She signaled for Murdock to settle in the corner of her office and remain quiet, then closed the door. Knew Murdock would tackle him as soon as the guy opened the door.

Hayley made it back into the closet in time to see the camera in the living room pick up the second prowler opening the front door. Her lips drew back in a snarl when he pulled his pistol from his holster, pause to look around, then tilt his head as if he detected her voice upstairs. She waited as he made his way up the stairs, the pistol aimed and ready for action.

Hayley got a better view of the handgun on the hall camera as he reached the top of the stairs, saw that it had a silencer on the end. He hesitated before stepping toward the closed office door. She stepped out of the closet, advanced across the soft carpet of her bedroom, grabbed the baseball bat she kept next to the door to the hall.

The prowler was so focused on her voice and the closed door to her office, he never heard Hayley rush behind him, whack him on the back of his head. He groaned, collapsed to the floor and was out cold.

Hayley was securing the guy's hands with zip ties when Liam rushed up the stairs.

Ten minutes later, Jack Collins waited while his deputies escorted the two men to their cruisers. He turned back to Liam who was nursing a bloody lip.

"Son, I'm running out of room in my jail."

"Sorry sir."

"If you ask me, the two of you are sitting ducks here. You've been lucky so far, but you might want to rethink things. You can't just sit here."

Jack turned to Hayley. "Does your father know about this latest attempt?"

"No, sir."

"I appreciate that you don't want to vacate your house, but this guy," he pointed to Liam, "can only do so much. You can't just sit here, fight them off one by one, wait for the final blow."

Hayley squirmed. The Sheriff was right. Whether she liked it or not, someone was still dictating her life. Restricting her movements. Imposing on her creative muse. Something needed to be done, she hadn't written a decent chapter in two days.

"I don't understand how the man can afford all this," Liam complained. "His accounts were frozen. No other secret accounts have been discovered." He cast a quick look at Hayley. "I've been debating going to the prison to interview him."

"Not a bad idea," Jack Collins agreed. "I guess I could put in a call to the warden."

Liam shook his head. "This isn't your responsibility, sir. Besides, I want to see the man for myself."

The sensor went off as soon as Brandon Anderson entered Gerard Turner's suite of offices. It was after five. Most days, Gerard Turner would still be holed up at his desk in his office but when Brandon got the call that he and the Assistant were attending a Board meeting in Atlanta, Brandon decided to make his move.

To be on the safe side in case the office was being surveilled, he had dressed in the navy uniform of the cleaning crew that had passed the background check and serviced the offices for the past five years. Pushing the big cart into the room, Brandon went through the motions of emptying the trash into the big tub, dusting the Assistant's desk, brushing his fingers under the ledge of the outer rim of the desk, the lamp. Found the mic under the keyboard of her computer. Another beneath the telephone.

Brandon's eyes narrowed as he pressed his lips together. Proved Liam's suspicion that someone monitored the office.

He found no other surveillance equipment, so he moved on to the boss' office.

Again, the sensor alerted, and Brandon was more concerned that someone had infiltrated the suite so deeply. Who could be doing it? Gone to all the trouble?

He went through the same motions – emptying trash, dusting the desk – in case there was a camera watching his every move. He discovered nothing out of the ordinary on the desk, checked the still signaling sensor.

He unloaded the portable vacuum, began cleaning the carpet while his eyes wandered the room, studied the molding. He straightened magazines on the end table next to the sofa in the informal alcove, dusted the pictures, spied the Ficus plant. Spotted the small camera tucked within the artificial grass at the base of the plant. Went through the motions of dusting the many leaves of the plant; smiled as he eased the plant around, so the camera was facing the dark corner of the office.

He installed his own camera on the top edge of the window facing the plant so he would catch whoever might stop by to readjust the plant.

Liam settled in the chair on the back deck. Enjoyed the quiet as he sipped his bourbon. Tossed the ball for Murdock who fetched and returned it with enthusiasm.

It had been a hell of a day and it wasn't over. He had a decision to make and wasn't sure Hayley would like it. There were too many unanswered questions, and somebody needed to get to the bottom of who put the hit on Hayley. And why now.

Had Ortiz been searching for her the entire time and made the connection with Savannah Hughes? If so, how did he connect Savannah with Hayley? Or Amelia Cox? Was Savannah seen with Gerard Turner somewhere? Did Ortiz know Hayley wrote under the name of Jillian McLeod.

How did they find out he and Hayley were in Boston on such short notice?

What sounded like a swarm of bees alerted him to look up, where he caught sight of the drone that zoomed over the house as Murdock raced up the steps with the ball.

"What the hell?" Liam fumed as he glared when the quadcopter doubled back and hovered in place as if challenging him. Like a mosquito debating where to bite.

Aggravated that they had now resorted to spying, Liam gripped the ball, aimed it at the device. Missed by inches because the drone bolted upward out of range.

While Murdock dashed after the misaimed ball, Liam studied the yard and patio, pretended to ignore the drone as it continued to hum, hover in place.

When Murdock returned with the ball, Liam aimed ahead of the drone while sprinting down the steps. He grabbed the hose Hayley used to water the flowers on the patio, aimed a full blast of water at the drone.

The drone shifted, tried to regain control but Liam continued to drench it until it fell to the ground. He raced over, stomped one of the propellers before the controller could regain command.

Liam doubted anyone would have the nerve to come forward and claim it. Decided he would turn it over to the Sheriff to be on the safe side.

He was turning the water off – would have to remind Hayley she needed to be more careful about leaving the water on, even though it worked in his favor this time – when his cell phone chimed.

"Did a sweep of the boss' office," Brandon started the conversation. "Found a bug on the Assistant's keyboard and phone. Camera in his office."

"Camera," Liam bellowed, "how the hell did that happen? Do we need to double check the cleaning crew?"

"No telling, I left everything as I found it. The camera was in the Ficus plant, so I turned it and it's now facing a blank wall. I installed a camera on the window across the room to monitor who comes in to change it."

"You need to give the cleaning crew a closer look. How the hell did someone manage to infiltrate the office so thoroughly? They're getting too technical. Just took down a drone."

"A drone," Brandon chuckled. "With all those tall trees? Yeah, I'm beginning to worry myself."

"I want to know where the money is coming from. His funds are frozen. It still doesn't explain how they knew we were in Boston. Any news on the new Assistant?"

"Still checking. Got a copy of the autopsy report on her husband. He was shot in the head with a high-powered rifle."

"Do you think it was an intentional hit?"

"No one has stepped forward to report an accidental shooting. Planning to research it more tomorrow."

"Be sure to check the cleaning crew as well," Liam ordered before ending the call.

"What's this?" Hayley studied the pile of mechanical parts.

"What's left of a drone. Another invasion of privacy. Another attempt to determine our whereabouts." He stuffed the pieces inside a black garbage bag. "Planning to drop it off at the Sheriff's office tomorrow on the way out of town."

"Out of town?" Hayley experienced a moment of panic. She'd finally gotten used to having him around. "You're going out of town?"

"Yes. You and I are going on another road trip."

Liam raised a hand when she started to object.

"Red, we need to find answers. For several reasons. Brandon called, said he found evidence your father's office has been infiltrated."

"My father? They're surveilling my father as well?"

"Yes. Brandon found two bugs on the Assistant's desk – on the phone, under the keyboard – and a camera in your father's office. Somebody's going to a lot of trouble and expense to find you. And hurt him. We need to do some damage control. Get some answers."

"By going out of town? Living on the run?" Hayley argued. "I will not let someone dictate my life ever again."

"We won't be running. I want to visit Ortiz. Put the fear of God in him. Let him know we're on to him."

"We're going to the prison?"

"I am. You're going to stay in a safe house where you'll be able to write while I research, interview, investigate, whatever needs to be done. I want you to go upstairs, pack your laptop, whatever you'll need for a week or so. Brandon has offered us a safe place to stay. We'll leave in an hour."

"But what about Murdock?"

"He'll go with us. Start earning his keep when I'm not around."

"But"

Liam grabbed her upper arms, gave her a good shake. "Red, Sheriff Collins was right when he said we can't sit here, wait for the final hit. I want closure as much as you do. I haven't told your father any of this yet, and until we find who is monitoring him, it'll stay that way."

"Okay. Okay," Hayley conceded, "I want it understood that wherever we go, it better have two bedrooms. Just because we're having sex, doesn't mean I plan to share your bed every night from now on."

Liam blinked. "You're thinking about sex at a time like this?"

Hayley felt her cheeks pinken."No, I'm not thinking about sex. I'm just setting the record straight. Don't get used to daily visits in my bed."

The corners of Liam's mouth turned up; his eyes gleamed.

"Sweetheart, I think you may have forgotten whose bed you woke up in this morning. You've got an hour to pack so get busy," he ordered as he headed around the corner of the house for the garage.

He was determined not to give her a chance for the last word.

Chapter Fourteen

They drove through the night. All Hayley could see was long twisting back roads lined with tall trees, flat gold reflectors down the center, at times, the interstate in the distance. They passed through small sleeping towns where businesses were closed and secured, houses dark as people rested up for another day.

She brushed her fingers across the necklace, sought its comfort. Thought of her father. Thankful that she'd been able to visit with him even though it was for only a few hours.

She leaned her head against the seat and sighed. She was exhausted. So much had happened – endless intruders, cameras and drones invading her privacy, long hours on the road to and from Boston, exhilarating evening dining and dancing, mind-boggling sex – and so little sleep. Was it thirty-six hours since they'd returned from Boston and now, they were on the road again.

Her thoughts drifted to Liam. He'd been back in her life for ten days and she'd gotten used to him being in the house, looked for him when he wasn't around, realized she needed his presence to stabilize her. Now that they had made love, would their relationship change? Would she become more dependent on him? Give him too much control?

Her mouth set in a hard line as she stared out the passenger window into the darkness. It angered her that once again William Ortiz was trying to turn her world upside down. But not this time, she gritted her teeth. This time she was stronger, healthier. Meaner and more resilient. Confident of herself. This time she would not be intimidated but determined to face her battles head on and be free of him.

She wondered what would happen once Ortiz was out of her life. When her life was normal again. When she wouldn't need Liam to protect her.

She leaned her forehead against the glass. Did she want him to stop protecting her was her last thought as she dozed off.

Liam let her sleep. Took advantage of the quiet to think. Too much was going on at once and the constant barrage of hitmen all focused on the bull's eye target plastered on Hayley's back concerned him.

He knew she was strong, invincible, but she could sustain only so much. She had her breaking point, and he worried her stamina, confidence might be slipping with each assault.

He was concerned that Brandon's security team had gotten sloppy. Gerard Turner's office had been infiltrated and they needed to discover who was behind it, how it was done. Did they have a mole in the organization?

There was little traffic on the road, but he couldn't help watching the rear-view mirror for a tail. Shadow.

It infuriated him that Hayley's life was turned upside down again. It all had to be tied to Savannah Hughes' murder. Somehow Ortiz had linked Savannah to Jillian McLeod, Hayley and Hayley's assumed name – Amelia Cox.

But how? And why for god's sake. The old man was in jail for the rest of his life, what good would it do him. It had to be more than vengeance behind this urgent need to end Hayley's life.

He wanted to confront the old man himself. It had to have cost him a small fortune for the army that had attempted to kill her. Where was the money coming from? His bank accounts were frozen, defunct.

The clear, cloudless pinkening sky, then the bright sun peeking through the tops of the trees on the long dense road promised a bright day. Liam checked the GPS which indicated they were eight miles from their destination. He yawned, lolled his head right and left, looked forward to getting settled in the cabin, catching some shut eye.

He rounded a curve, and it seemed the world brightened. There was life as they approached open fields and houses ahead of a small town.

He sensed Hayley awakening, heard his stomach grumble in hunger, was sure Murdock needed to stop to pee. Deciding now might be a good stopping point, he pulled into the parking lot of the restaurant. A full lot guaranteed it was the local favorite.

"We're less than eight miles out," he said when Hayley straightened in her seat. "Maybe we can check out the local restaurant, get something to eat before heading to the cabin."

They let Murdock relieve himself, roam the edge of the parking lot, relieve himself some more before giving him some water and leaving a bowl of food in the truck.

The door to the restaurant jingled when they stepped inside. Conversation stopped as heads turned to check them out then resumed talking when Liam led Hayley to a table in the center of the room.

Hayley tensed that they were so exposed, would have preferred a booth or corner table but the room was small – six tables and a counter bar – and the place was packed. Most were men of all ages and sizes dressed in rugged wear. She decided they must be construction workers or loggers considering their bright vests and steel toe boots.

Three young women sat around one table enjoying coffee while two babies slept in their strollers on the side. Hayley figured they might be young mothers getting together after dropping their children off a school.

Two waitresses circulated the room, taking orders, serving meals, refilling drinks. One was young, mid-thirties, the other late fifties, early sixties. Hayley wondered if they might be mother and daughter as they shared the same features – narrow faces, brown eyes, pointed noses, full lips that broke into expressive smiles. They were both blonde, the younger one wore her hair in a ponytail, the other in a bun on top of her head. Tall, slender and full of energy, she was certain they were local as they chatted with the customers.

Hayley and Liam ordered hearty breakfasts as it had been a long night full of worry and stress.

"This is such a small town," Hayley commented to the older waitress as she refilled her coffee. "Nice and quaint. What do you do in case of emergencies?"

"The hospital is in the next town over, twenty miles away. Of course, we have what we need here – doctor, drug store, grocery store, bank. We enjoy the quiet. No sirens, hotrodders, shootings."

"Do you get many visitors?" Liam inquired.

"Like you, good looking?" She cackled at his pinkened cheeks. "We get our fair amount of people passing through. You passing through?"

"We're visiting a friend outside of town."

The waitress gave him a speculative eye. "Wouldn't be Brandon Anderson, would it?"

Liam blinked. "As a matter of fact, it is. You know Brandon?"

She smiled. "He used to come in here a lot when they were building his house. Doted over that place like it was his mistress. Slept there during the construction. I'm going to be upset if he's there now and hasn't stopped in to see me."

"No, he's on assignment," Liam assured her. "He offered it to us for a few days."

"You must be good friends for him to let you stay without him. Like I said, he was very protective of that place. Tell him Mable said hi the next time you talk to him."

As they left the restaurant, Liam regarded the mom-and-pop grocery store across the road.

"Brandon said the shelves and fridge are bare. We should stock up on food for the next few days. The less we're seen around town the better."

It was an old country store in an old frame building with wide windows on each side of the entrance, steps up to the double doors that creaked then jingled a bell whenever anyone entered. Inside were wide plank floors, deep wooden shelves, handmade signs tacked above the shelves, prices affixed to the items on bright red stickers.

Hayley wondered if she'd stepped back in time.

Liam stopped in his tracks. "Didn't I just see you in the restaurant?" He commented to the woman at the check-out counter who was the mirror image of Mable. Upon closer examination, he realized while Mable's hair had been gathered in a knot on top of her head, this woman's hair was short, cropped to the shape of her face.

The woman chuckled. "I'm Maude. You must be talking about my twin sister."

Liam returned her smile as he wandered over to the small bakery section on the left of the door, studied the large glass case displaying cookies, pies, cakes and donuts. A single café table and two chairs was set in front of the big open window, a tall cabinet with canteens of coffee, Styrofoam cups and lids, napkins, flavored creamers and sugar fixings in the corner against the side wall.

Down from the bakery was a long meat counter with waist high deli case full of fresh meats – beef steaks, chicken, pork chops and roasts, small selection of fish. Next to it was a smaller deli case of cheeses and yogurts.

A modest size kitchen stretched across the back of the room with a commercial grill, fryer and oven. Another long narrow counter and condiment station separated it from the main room. The store offered prepared foods to go from the counter and a sliding glass window on the side of the building. Hayley sniffed beef and onions grilling; studied the menu that offered hamburgers, barbeque, hot dogs. Today's special was brisket.

Hayley stared out the window, saw two people seated at a picnic table eating breakfast sandwiches.

Considering it wasn't even nine in the morning, a fair number of people were shopping the shelves. Two older ladies were deep in conversation off to one side while others strolled the five narrow aisles, inspected the small selection of wines.

She and Liam each grabbed a red hand basket.

Liam filled his with chips, peanuts, crackers, bread and peanut butter and jelly before he wandered over to the bakery case for a closer look.

Hayley's overflowed with half dozen box of eggs, apples, chicken breasts, cheese, milk and yogurt. Deciding their meals might need to be simple, she grabbed a can of cream of celery soup, box of rice for the chicken. She plucked an Italian loaf of bread from the bread shelf to serve with the lasagna dish she'd grabbed out of the freezer before they left.

"We also have a vegetable stand on the edge of town," the butcher suggested when he glimpsed her healthy items.

On the way to the checkout counter, she reached for a bag of dog treats for Murdock and was thankful they'd brought his dog food as there wasn't much room in the basket.

Liam nudged Hayley with an elbow, nodded his head toward the selection of books near the check-out counter. Hayley smiled when she glanced over, spied the bright blue cover of her latest book displayed front and center on the display.

"I like your selection of books," Liam complimented Maude as he set his basket on the counter.

"Why thank you. We just got the new Jillian McLeod books yesterday. Bought my copy and was up till two this morning reading it." She performed an exaggerated shiver as she scanned his chips. "She sure can describe a murder scene."

Hayley hoped Maude didn't notice her pinkened cheeks as she beamed inside with pride. Other than the infrequent comments, reviews and sales reports, she had no idea what her readers thought of her books. Or how many readers she had. Unlike other authors who had Facebook pages for readers to gush over their books, her forced anonymity had prevented such interaction with the public.

"Yeah," Liam agreed. "I've read a couple of her books myself. Wondered if she thinks of a certain person when she kills her victims."

The clerk cackled. "I know." She waved a hand in agreement. "She's so descriptive. I caught myself wincing a couple times last night. But I love her books. Wish I could meet her; ask her how she comes up with her stories. Tell her how much I like her books. They don't say too much about her on the jacket."

The clerk scanned his last item, hesitated when she eyeballed Hayley's overflowing basket.

"You two together?"

Liam nodded, started handing her some of the items.

"I've got it, honey." She waved to him. "You two new to the area?" She inquired as she weighed Hayley's apples.

"Just passing through. Staying in a small cabin in the woods for a few days."

The woman looked up, studied him. "The only person I know with a small cabin in this area is Brandon Anderson."

"You know Brandon?"

"Honey, I think everybody knows Brandon. He was the talk of the town when he was building that place. Now that it's finished, we don't see hide nor hair of him. Can't figure that out. Got the job done then he disappeared!"

"Brandon stays pretty busy," Liam defended his friend.

Maude scanned Murdock's treats. "I see you have a dog. Need to be careful. We've had a few bear sightings these past few weeks."

"Now you can say you've met one of your fans." Liam complimented Hayley as he put the bagged groceries on the back seat next to Murdock.

They drove through the small town, past the *Truist* bank branch, post office. Turned off the main road to travel several miles up the mountain. Although there was no mailbox or indication of a house through the woods, Liam turned onto the narrow drive that snaked further into the hills.

The drive was longer than her own, ended at a small yard that still needed landscaping. Liam parked near the five steps that led up to the front porch that spread across the middle section of the cabin. Two double-wide windows and a single narrow window were designed into the extended house on each side of the porch.

The porch was bare except for the four cedar columns, two on each side of the steps. Hayley imagined rocking chairs; flowerpots filled with bright flowers decorating the entrance.

Double doors opened into a large square great room with kitchen on the left, separated from the living area by a long bar and five stools. The sparse room contained a long leather sofa facing the fireplace, single matching leather recliner, flat screen TV over the mantle, built in oak bookcases on either side of the fireplace. There was a vintage oak counter height dining table and four chairs in one corner off from the kitchen where Hayley set her laptop.

The kitchen was equipped with a slate French door refrigerator, stove, and microwave; cream color custom made slatted cabinets surrounded the appliances. The bar featured a farmhouse sink, dishwasher and cream and slate Formica counter with a raised lip and counter for eating at the stools on the entertainment side.

Various scatter rugs covered the wide plank laminate floors. Another set of double doors led to a porch that spanned the back of the house.

Doors opened to four bedrooms on each corner of the great room. Two of the bedrooms were empty of furniture. The third held a big queen size bed, nightstand on one side, closet on the left. Chair at the foot of the bed. Twin beds were in the fourth bedroom. Each bedroom hosted its own bathroom with a glassed shower, long counter with one sink.

There were no windows on the sides of the cabin, only one window in each of the bedrooms.

Liam checked the windows, closed the blinds and doors to the empty bedrooms for security. Did the same for the other two after depositing a bag with sheets and towels on the queen size bed.

Hayley studied the view from the doors to the back porch that looked out on the thick woods and yard waiting to be seeded and landscaped. Brandon had put a lot of thought into the design of his cabin in the woods and she wondered if he had even stayed here. Felt guilty about staying in Brandon's new home away from home. She checked the kitchen cabinets and found four plates, four knives, forks and spoons, two pots, and one frying pan. The essentials.

They unloaded the truck, put the groceries away, decided to hike the woods. Give Murdock a chance to exercise. Get familiar with the area as Liam wanted to check the terrain, be prepared in case of future attacks.

"Do you think they will find us here?" Hayley questioned his paranoia.

"They found us in Boston, didn't they?"

Hayley was exhausted when she went to bed that evening. After hiking the woods and consuming her share of a bottle of zinfandel wine with the lasagna, she decided to call it a night.

She didn't question the lack of sheets for the twin beds, simply made the queen size bed, climbed beneath the covers, hoped to fall into a deep sleep. Prayed the wine would prevent her mind from rehashing the last assault at the house.

Realized she had become dependent on the cameras she had resisted in the beginning to watch and protect her. Worried there were no cameras in Brandon's woods as she snuggled into the covers and closed her eyes.

Suddenly, she was tossing and turning imagining cameras watching her, flashing at her every step, blinding her from leaving. She kept hearing the clicking of locks every door she tried to escape the man who was staring down at Judith's lifeless body while he talked to someone on his phone.

"It's done." Hayley heard him say.

She must have made a noise because all of a sudden, the man turned, stared at her. Then came for her.

Hayley found herself screaming before her world turned black.

Angry male voices awakened her, and she realized another man was in the apartment. She couldn't move, her body hurt all over. She kept her eyes closed for fear they would beat her more. She listened to them talk, the one man screamed, "You've got two dead bodies and no evidence! Where's the evidence," he demanded.

Hayley opened her eyes, glimpsed the men as they turned to leave. When she was certain she was alone, she crawled to her phone, passed out as soon as she dialed nine-one-one.

Was this the man trying to kill her because he fears she can blow his cover?

Hayley awakened in a panic and screamed.

Liam had been reading when Hayley decided to go to bed. He knew she was tired, decided to let her relax, settle into sleep before he joined her.

He had just dozed off on the sofa when her blood curdling scream caused him to jackknife of the sofa. He rushed into the bedroom, gathered her close when she jumped into his arms. He rocked her, rubbed his hand up and down her arm trying to console her.

"It's okay, you're safe here."

"Will I ever be safe?" Hayley sobbed into the curve of his neck. "Anywhere?"

"I'll get the bastard, I promise."

"Promise?" She begged with a sleepy slur.

He shifted, lay beside her, pulled the blanket over them as he continued to hold her close. Felt her settle into his side, rubbed his fingers up and down her arm, trying to sooth the tense muscles, calm the fears, settle the nerves. Within minutes, she was relaxed, let out a contented sigh as she wrapped an arm around his middle, snuggled next to him.

Liam rested his head against the pillow, stared at the ceiling, vowed the end to her worries would come soon.

Chapter Fifteen

Liam studied the long, imposing maximum security prison that housed some of the most dangerous criminals in history. Concrete walls thirty feet high and what looked like a quarter mile long stood solid and impenetrable. He had analyzed the blueprints of the facility, understood the architecture was repeated on the back side so the concrete walls surrounded its guests. Caged them with no possible means for escape. Offered only a limited inner corral for exercise or recreation.

A large tower in the center on the front served as the entrance. Smaller towers midway down and at each corner of the facility served as observation points of the surrounding property and inner courtyard, camera surveillance of the halls and prison cells.

Two flags – American and the State of New York – flittered in the breeze from tall poles in the small quadrangle half-way down the front lawn. Blacktop pavement circled the lawn, flowed into large staff and visitor parking lots ranged across the front of the prison.

The prison offered no windows. The inmates gave up the freedom to fresh air, healthy food and liberty when they committed their crime.

He stashed his weapon in the console beneath his hat. He had the permit to carry, just didn't see the need to draw any more attention to himself than necessary.

He stepped inside the entrance where he was greeted by uniformed armed guards, a security checkpoint and a logbook. Brandon had scheduled the appointment and Liam was thankful his up-to-date clearance speeded up the processing of his visit with the warden.

After logging in, a female guard escorted him through another pair of locked doors, down a long hall, past smaller offices where he perceived civilians and officers of the law working at desks, talking on their phones, monitoring screens. She knocked at a wide panel door that opened into a bright room lit by a long line of windows that overlooked the interior courtyard of the facility. Liam glimpsed inmates walking, jogging, exercising in fenced areas, shooting basketball in another.

Brandon had emailed him the specifics about the warden, Tom Donovan, who had worked his way up from New York City beat cop to guard at Rikers then here where he'd been warden for ten years. Liam also understood Donovan looked forward to retirement in two years.

The warden stood at three inches over six feet, had fading ginger hair and a round Irish face. He was a stout man with brawny shoulders, a solid chest, stocky arms and rounded stomach. Liam doubted any prisoner would dare to venture past him if he were guarding the front gates.

Tom Donovan had pulled and reviewed the file on William Ortiz and after greeting and motioning Liam to sit, leaned back in his chair, steepled his hands over his stomach to study the young man who'd shown interest in one of his inmates.

"Are you family, Mr. Walker?"

"No, sir. Just a concerned citizen."

Liam preferred not to divulge any more information than necessary. The Warden might project the imposing figurehead, but Liam wasn't certain how much control Ortiz might have in the prison.

"I see from his file here he has no family listed. Considering his current condition, mind if I ask why the concern."

"Current condition?" Liam jerked, spoke out of the side of his mouth.

"Yes," the warden sat upright, flipped through the file. "It seems he was attacked last year. A guard found him unconscious in his cell with a stab wound. He was taken to the infirmary and treated. Stayed for several days but while there they decided to do some tests when he showed signs of significant confusion. Some dementia. He was relocated to the mental health hall for his protection."

Liam studied the warden. "So, you're saying William Ortiz has Alzheimer's?"

"That's what the medical papers document. I haven't seen him personally."

Liam shook his head in disbelief. Decided this mystery got stranger by the minute.

"Is it possible for me to see him?"

"Maybe," Tom Donovan noted Liam's reaction. "But first I need to understand the extent of your interest. He hasn't had any visitors since he arrived here. Why this sudden interest?"

Liam considered the warden's poker face. Realized he was at a disadvantage and unless he came clean didn't see the warden cooperating. Decided he'd risk it.

"William Ortiz was convicted of the murder of Judith Toliver and attempted murder of Hayley Turner five years ago. I'm here on behalf of Hayley Turner. There have been several attempts in recent weeks on her life and I am trying to determine who might have ordered those hits."

The warden scanned through the file further, reviewed the names associated with the case.

"This confirms all you've said. He murdered Judith Toliver, attempted to murder Hayley Turner." He looked up. "And Ms. Turner is the lady you represent?"

Liam nodded. "Ms. Turner has been in my protective custody for the past five years. Since the trial that convicted William Ortiz. She has had five attempts on her life in the past two weeks. I am hoping to confirm whether William Ortiz has placed a bounty on her. If not him, who."

"I'm sorry Ms. Turner is having this problem but reading over Ortiz's file, I have to doubt his mental capacity to orchestrate such hits. He has been solitarily confined to the mental ward for the past six months. I will be glad to have you escorted to his cell to confirm that."

"Thank you, sir. That's all I can ask at this time."

Both men stood.

"You know, I don't get involved in cases such as this, but you do have my curiosity up." He brushed a hand across his round belly, adjusted his belt. "I've got some time this morning, a good long walk would probably do me some good."

It was indeed a long walk down narrow halls with painted pale green walls. Their footsteps echoed on the light and dark green speckled floor tiles that were clean but showed the wear of age. Liam perused their reflections in the bubble mirrors as they rounded the intersection of halls at the far corner of the facility.

Donovan coded them through two secured metal doors into the minimum security, mental health wing of the prison. Liam registered the metallic sound of the doors closing behind them, picked up on the sterile, antiseptic hospital odor.

They continued down another long hall, stopped in front of a door with a small window insert that overlooked the interior of the small room.

Liam leaned over, observed the narrow hospital bed next to the wall. There was no other furniture other than a small commode chair, smaller barred window.

He thought it odd that prisoners facing years of confinement were denied glimpses of the outside world yet those with limited life capacity were offered a small glimpse of what they would soon be missing.

Liam shook his head as he considered the lone occupant, recognized William Ortiz dressed in the drab prison uniform, confined to a wheelchair. Unlike the well-dressed angry man that had been sentenced five years earlier, his shoulders were slumped as he stared off into space, his arms strapped to the chair.

"Can I help you, Warden?" A nurse stepped toward them from a small office further down the hall.

"Mr. Ortiz has a visitor. We were just checking on his condition."

The nurse frowned, cast a consoling look toward Liam. Assumed he was a concerned family member.

"Unfortunately, he just sits in his wheelchair. It has gotten to the point where we must feed him, get him up to walk the hall once each day. He doesn't talk and has had no visitors since he was brought here."

"You're certain he has had no visitors?" Liam inquired.

He leaped out of his chair, paced the room after reading the email from his source at the prison. Sweat trickled down his spine as he rammed his fists into his pants pockets, troubled that Walker now knows about the dementia. That the old man couldn't pee by himself much less plan all the attacks on the bitch.

Now they will start investigating who is really behind all the hits.

Anger roared through him. He didn't know who he hated more. Walker for snooping too much or the bitch for all her meddling.

Now they will start snooping again. It was supposed to be a simple random hit. Staged suicide. His revenge so he could move on with his life.

Now he'd be looking over his shoulder, worried she'd remember, blow his cover.

He was furious they would start asking questions, look at the loose ends they let slip through the cracks before. Start putting the pieces together.

He needed to keep better tabs on his other source. Be prepared for the next hit. Make sure the source didn't lead them back to him.

His mouth twisted. They might think they were getting close, but he was two steps ahead. In fact, things were already in place. They'd soon learn their days were numbered. He was closer than they thought.

While Liam was studying William Ortiz, Hayley was going stir crazy. She'd intended to write but Faith and Kyle wouldn't talk to her. Instead, she found herself wandering the cabin, peeking out the windows.

She missed the familiar surroundings of her office, the books and resources she'd decided not to pack for such a short trip.

She'd gotten used to the cameras in the woods at home. Going to her secret stairwell to check them from time to time. Now, she didn't know if anyone was outside spying on her, trying to get closer for a shot. She kept vigil for any vehicle that might drive up the front drive.

She wasn't getting paranoid but worried about Liam having their only means of transportation. What if someone should wander up to the cabin?

She recalled their conversation that morning before he'd left.

"Red, we're in the middle of nowhere. We left in the dead of night. There's no way they could have tracked us."

"That's what you said about Boston and look what that got us."

"This is Brandon's hideaway. No one knows about it. I didn't even know about it until he offered it to me."

"Are you sure? Someone could be watching Brandon," she'd exclaimed throwing her hands in the air as she paced. "They could be tracking Brandon's calls."

Last night's nightmare was still fresh on her mind. She wondered why she should suddenly dream of a second man. Did something trigger it? Was some of the amnesia she'd experienced beginning to clear? Was she remembering facts she'd blocked out before?

Had there been a second man who was now orchestrating her demise?

Liam was pondering the same thing as he travelled back to the cabin.

It was obvious the William Ortiz he visited in the prison did not have the mental capacity to orchestrate all the hits he and Hayley had experienced these past few weeks.

Nor the money.

Someone was masterminding the assassination attempts. He just needed to determine who. Who had the most at stake in the incident? The organization had been disintegrated. The son was presumed to be dead. The only other family was the nephew who was dating Judith Toliver.

He decided to give Brandon a call on the way back to the cabin.

"There is no way William Ortiz could have orchestrated those hits. He's locked up in a tiny cell, strapped to a wheelchair. Brandon, the man's a basket case. Has Alzheimer's."

"Are you serious?" Brandon amazed.

"Saw him with my own eyes. Warden says no one has visited him since he set foot in the place. He was attacked last year, transferred to the infirmary. That's when they diagnosed him with the dementia, moved him to the mental health section."

Liam studied the rearview mirror when the sun's rays reflected off a pale blue sedan in the distance behind him. He felt an itch between his shoulder blades as he debated how long it had been following him. Breathed a sigh of relief when the car turned off the road.

"Any developments in the security breach of the boss' office?"

"Nothing yet," Brandon answered.

"Then I guess we're back to square one. What do you have on the nephew?"

"Not much. He disappeared after the trial, but I tracked him to Clippersville."

"Clippersville, New York?"

"Yeah, small town about fifty miles west of the cabin. He manages a small bank there."

Liam debated detouring to the town but was overdue getting back to Hayley. Knew she wouldn't be happy with him as it was. Less understanding if he took another side trip.

"I want to talk to him, but I need to get back to Hayley. She's been alone at the cabin all day. I'm surprised my cell phone hasn't been ringing before now."

"Want me to arrange a meeting with the nephew?"

"Couldn't hurt. Give me a chance to feel him out. If he's not involved, he might give us a lead."

As expected, Liam drove up the long drive to find Hayley pacing the front porch.

"No luck with Ortiz. He's holed up in a prison cell with Alzheimer's."

Hayley stared at him in disbelief.

"I'm going to meet the nephew tomorrow."

"Sebastian? You're going to interview Sebastian?"

"Yes," Liam nodded his head. "He disappeared after the trial, but Brandon located him in a small town about fifty miles from here. Manages a bank there. I have an appointment to discuss a home mortgage with him tomorrow."

"Mortgage, huh?"

"Using an assumed name. Don't want him to rabbit before I can talk to him."

"I'm going with you," Hayley decided. She turned to go inside the cabin, refused to give him the opportunity to object.

Liam followed her inside the cabin. "Red, I don't think that's a good idea."

"I don't care," she threw her hands in the air. "I thought I would go stir-crazy today. This place is nice, but I can't concentrate. Not like I can at home. Then I was worried about who would be outside, watching me."

"I told you, there's no way they can track us here."

"You don't know that. Look what happened in Boston. I don't care. I'm going."

"You don't have anything suitable to wear."

"Like you brought your best suit along?" Hayley countered; her hands fisted on her hips. "Liam it's not like we're going to ask for a real loan. All we need to do is be presentable. Once we're in his office, we ask questions."

"I still don't want you so exposed."

"I have my blonde wig. He won't even recognize me."

Liam shut his eyes, clenched his jaw in frustration. Realized he needed to try another tactic. He had no idea how involved Sebastian Ortiz was with the family. Whether he even had anything to do with the murder. He didn't want to expose Hayley any more than necessary.

"Hayley," he stepped toward her, brushed his hands up and down her upper arms as he stared into her smoky green eyes. "I'm trying to look out for your well-being. We've been lucky so far; I can't afford to expose you. I care about you." He leaned forward to brush her lips with his. "We need to be careful."

His teeth nibbled the side of her jaw, his nose skirted down her long neck.

Hayley shivered at the warm breath, soft bristles of his beard, wet tongue that circled her earlobe.

Suspicious of his change in tactics, she decided two could play this game.

She leaned into him, curled her hands around his shoulders, glided them to his neck, threaded her fingers through his hair.

"Much as I hate to admit it, I care about you as well."

When Liam lifted his head in surprise, she edged closer, captured his lips with hers. Her tongue sought his, twined and twirled as she nudged her body against his, deepened the kiss.

Liam's body came alive with each assault of her tongue. Throbbed with each thrust of her breasts against his chest. His hands curled around her bottom, pressed her against his iron-hard arousal.

Hayley smiled to herself, decided she needed to put this in one of her books. She was so focused on the actions, imagining the descriptive words, she registered too late that he had undone her jeans, ventured further.

She gasped, bucked when his fingers caressed her warm center, almost collapsed from the orgasm that cascaded through her. She intensified the kiss as his fingers continued to stroke her.

When he realized he needed release, Liam carried her into the bedroom.

Lips still locked, they quickly disposed of their clothes, fell onto the bed.

She reached for him, but he trapped her arms above her head as he straddled her, his mouth skimmed over her shoulders. Her breath hitched when his mouth came down on her breast, her feet digging into the mattress as she offered her body to him.

Liam hummed at the temptress beneath him. Foraged that long slim body that had tempted him for so long. Every inch of him craved her as he skimmed her waist, hip, worked his way along her inner thigh to the very core of her being.

Hayley felt dizzy, weightless, her senses so focused on the tip of his nose, warm breath that seemed to devour her body; awaited the onset of his sensuous mouth. One second, she was relaxed as if tranquilized, the next she jerked when he shifted her hips and feasted.

Liam shifted over her, renewed her pleasure as he eased inside her. Penetrated deeper and deeper with each hammering thrust until the intoxicating heat crested and he emptied into her.

They lay back on the bed, giving their bodies a chance to cool, hearts to settle, breathing to steady. Both stared at the ceiling and smiled. Each convinced they'd won their battle.

"Liam," Hayley murmured.

"Hmm," Liam responded, content, satisfied.

"I'm still going with you tomorrow."

Chapter Sixteen

Hayley wound her long braid around her head, plopped the blonde wig atop her hair and arranged the tresses about her face and shoulders. She made a face at her new look, decided green eyes and blonde hair just weren't the fashion. Wished she had some brown contacts.

She smiled as she recalled her battle of wills with Liam the evening before. Even after being ravished, she'd stood up to him, held her ground, insisted she was going with him.

And won.

She took extra care with her makeup because she needed to be incognito. Worried Sebastian Ortiz might recognize her. After all, he had dated Judith for six months before she was murdered. Deep down, she'd like Sebastian, thought he was good for Judith. Had even accompanied them to a couple movies.

Until they could determine the extent of Sebastian's involvement in his uncle's organization, she needed to be anonymous.

Liam studied Hayley when she sauntered out of the bedroom. Hoped Sebastian had a short memory as the black slacks and royal blue sweater did little to disguise her sleek trim figure. He studied her face and except for the daring bold look, he saw no resemblance to the bewitching woman he'd pleasured yesterday.

Dressed in the dark jeans and gray sweater he'd arrived at her house in, he was still uptight that she'd managed to outwit him. He'd debated sneaking out while she dressed but decided she'd never forgive him, make his life miserable if he had.

It was her life that was on the line. She was as committed to finding answers and deserved to be in on the interview. They would take extra precautions.

During the trip to the bank, Hayley shared what little she knew of Sebastian Ortiz.

"He was a likeable guy, always friendly, pleasant. He was an auditor, worked in one of the banks. I think he wanted Judith to leave her job. I remember he was always telling her about openings at the bank. But she preferred the bookkeeping side, working for an established business. Until those last few months before she was murdered.

"Judith was aware that Sebastian was William Ortiz's nephew, but I don't know how close he was to his uncle. He never talked about the family."

Liam studied the pale blue sedan in the rearview mirror. Thought about the one from the day before, recalled the nagging itch between his shoulders. Since it had been tailing them since they left the town, he eased up on the throttle to let it come closer. It turned off the main road but not before Liam detected two black stripes on the passenger side door. He wondered if the car had been side-swiped. Or side swiped another car.

They arrived in Clippersville thirty minutes ahead of their appointment. Liam wanted to watch the comings and goings of the bank. Gauge the activity. It was a small branch with the main entry on the main street, small parking lot, drive-thru window and second entry on the back of the building.

Brandon had scheduled a late afternoon appointment. Figured if it was close to closing time, there would be a minimum of customers in the bank, less interruptions should the discussion be worthwhile.

The bank itself was a large open room with two offices sectioned off with a door and doublewide window overlooking the main room on the right, a long counter with three teller stations on the left. The receptionist sat in the middle of the room at a L-shaped desk outside the office closest to the front entrance.

Liam approached the receptionist desk, stated their fictitious names and appointment time.

Hayley recognized Sebastian right away. He sat behind his desk, talked with an easy calm manner on the phone. She recalled he was average height, on the thin side with wiry shoulders. He wasn't into fitness and juggled numbers; the telephone receiver was probably the heaviest of his weights. He had an oblong, cleanshaven face, his ash brown hair was combed and parted to the right.

The receptionist said Mr. Ortiz would be with them in a moment, offered them glass of water, soda or coffee while they waited.

Liam and Hayley declined, settled on the embroidered loveseat opposite the door to his office.

Minutes later, Sebastian rose, cleared his desk, stepped out of his office toward them.

Liam experienced a slight prick of worry when he picked up on a slight hesitation in Sebastian's step as he approached, offered his hand. The banker gave Hayley a sharp look before leading them into his office, shutting the door behind them.

It wasn't a large office. The wide mahogany desk took up a good portion of the space with sufficient room for his side of the desk, just enough legroom for the leather round backed visitor chairs backed to the large paned window that looked out on the main room. His desktop computer rested on the tall credenza to his left, telephone, notepad, business card and pen holders on the shining desk between them.

Hayley studied the night deposit vault mounted in the wall in the corner. Guessed his first order of business was to count the money dropped there the night before. That or hand it over to one of the tellers.

"So, you would like to get pre-qualified for a home?" Sebastian sat back in his chair and smiled. "Will you be buying locally?"

Liam leaned back, bounced a knee as he took a moment to gauge the banker. "Actually, we're here on another matter."

Sebastian frowned. "But I thought,"

"I'll get right to the point," Liam spoke from the side of his mouth as he shifted, rested his elbows on the rounded arms of his chair. "I understand you have an uncle named William Ortiz."

Sebastian stiffened. Looked beyond them for his receptionist who was seated outside his office.

He cleared his throat, sat upright. "Yes. I have an uncle named William Ortiz. I don't claim him. Haven't seen him in over five years."

"Because he is in prison." Liam stated.

Sebastian loosened the tie that was choking him. "Yes. And I've had nothing to do with him since his trial."

"Were you aware he suffers from Alzheimer's?"

Sebastian blinked. "No, I did not. Like I said I've had nothing to do with him since the trial. He murdered a dear friend of mine."

"Judith Toliver."

Sebastian glanced at Hayley, frowned, returned his gaze to Liam.

"Yes, I was in love with her. Devastated when she was murdered. Look," Sebastian shifted, leaned toward them, "my uncle was much older than my father and I guess you could say he was the black sheep of the family. I wasn't happy about Judith working for him and tried more than once to get her to quit. Particularly when she told me about some of her concerns."

Sebastian angled his head toward Hayley, his brown eyes narrowed as he studied her green ones.

"Hayley? Is that you?"

Hayley jerked when he spoke her name. She had remained silent. Let Liam do all the talking.

"It *is* you," Sebastian confirmed. "It's your eyes. I'd recognize them anywhere." He leaned closer, stared into her eyes. "I want you to know I was devastated to hear of Judith's murder and more shocked that you had been beaten. And when you came forward at my uncle's trial, I felt nothing but relief that the monster would pay for what he did to Judith."

Sebastian turned back to Liam.

"My uncle was a vicious man in his younger years and the fact that he now has Alzheimer's seems so fitting. But what is most upsetting, my cousin was worse."

"Cousin?"

"Yes, my uncle's son. Simon Ortiz."

"Do you know where this son might be?"

Sebastian shrugged a shoulder. "No idea. He was supposedly killed in a boating accident several months before Judith's murder."

"Supposedly?" Liam asked.

Sebastian nodded his head. "Went on some fishing trip. I understand there was an explosion, and they never found his body."

"I don't suppose you have any pictures of your cousin?"

"No. After the trial, my family pretty much disowned my uncle. Simon and I grew up together, but we were never close. Sorry."

Sebastian Ortiz leaned back in his chair, stared as if in a trance across the lobby. It was after seven, the bank was empty. Ever since Hayley's visit and the blast from the past, he'd been unable to concentrate. He'd sat for over an hour reliving Judith's murder all over again.

Regretted not taking action to warn her about his uncle when she'd expressed her concerns. Sorry he hadn't protected her more. He recalled the heartbreak when he'd learned of Judith's murder, anguish during the trial, amazement at Hayley's surprise appearance in the courtroom and exposure of his uncle's vicious organization.

It had taken him over a year to grieve, reconcile to Judith's murder. Decide to make a clean break and accept the position here. It had taken another year before he'd learned to live again. Finally met a woman who brought joy into his life.

He checked his phone and frowned to see he had a missed call from Becky. Recalled their plans for the evening.

He dialed her number, waited for her to answer while he set the bank's alarm, locked the doors. Stepped toward his car parked across the parking lot.

"Sebastian," two voices spoke at the same time. He smiled at Becky's excited voice on the phone, looked over in puzzlement at the male voice calling from inside the blue car with the two black stripes on the passenger door.

Sebastian jerked when the silent bullet struck him in the middle of his chest.

Hayley and Liam grabbed a quick dinner in the restaurant before returning to the cabin and started researching Simon Ortiz.

Liam talked with his contact with the New York police, shared the information with Brandon.

"Seems the son had the typical boyhood scrapes considering the family background – breaking and entering, drunk and disorderly, trashed a bar. Then it looks like he straightened up. Maybe the father cracked the whip, used the belt, started grooming him for the business. He went to college, quit his senior year, went to work with his father. Never married.

"Five, six years ago he was still working the business and one evening he went out in the boat. There was a storm, boat turned up on shore a couple days later, no sign of him. He was never found. Presumed dead.

"Weeks later, Judith Toliver was murdered. I guess he got lost in the news during the trial," Liam concluded.

Did he really disappear? Liam wondered.

While Liam and Brandon discussed Simon Ortiz's background, Hayley googled the accident, clicked on articles about the accident, confirmed they never found the body.

She studied the article.

The Coast Guard is piecing through fiberglass and metal debris of "Can't Catch Me" seeking an explanation for the mysterious disappearance of Simon James Ortiz. His body has not been found and it is feared he drifted out to sea.

According to his family, he was due at the celebration of his father's eightieth birthday later that evening and was reported missing the following morning.

There were no witnesses, and they cannot determine the cause although it is believed he was flung overboard but there are still many unanswered questions.

The Coast Guard received the report, conducted boat and helicopter searches for over forty-eight hours, covering over five thousand nautical miles. The search has been discontinued but the Coast Guard continues to investigate.

Hayley studied the fuzzy head shot of Simon Ortiz. His face was oblong, with high cheeks and dark hair and full moustache above his top lip. It was his piercing dark eyes and arrogant expression that shook her as she focused her phone to take a picture.

"That means he might still be alive," Hayley commented minutes later as she filled their wine glasses. "Do you suppose he might have been the second man I saw the night Judith was murdered?"

When Liam didn't answer, she looked up, found him staring at the silent TV screen.

It was after eleven and the local news was broadcasting the late news. Hayley's mouth fell open when she recognized the picture of Sebastian Ortiz.

Liam grabbed for the remote, turned up the volume.

"We have just received word of a shooting at the Clippersville National Bank. Sebastian Ortiz, branch manager there was found shot in the bank's parking lot. He had apparently been on the phone with a friend when he was gunned down. Ortiz had been with the bank for three years and was well liked in the community. Police are investigating the incident and ask that anyone who might have any helpful information to please contact them via their anonymous tipline."

Hayley stopped in her tracks, stared at the TV in disbelief.

"What did we do? Did we cause that? Liam?"

Liam turned to see that Hayley's face was deathly white. His gaze fell to her chest, recognized the red beam of a sighted gun.

Chapter Seventeen

Murdock barked with furor as he raced to the front door the same moment Liam tackled Hayley to the floor. Wine splashed, glasses shattered, and Hayley landed on her side, banged her head against the oak bookcase next to the fireplace.

Liam grabbed for the lamp cord, yanked it from the wall socket before he scurried across the floor to the wall switch next to the front door. Reached up to flip the switch pitching the cabin into darkness.

His quick actions had prevented the intruder from taking his shot but that didn't mean there wouldn't be a second attempt. It only bought them a little time.

He shushed the dog, crawled back toward the fireplace to find Hayley still lying on the floor, her hand rubbing the side of her head.

"Are you okay?"

"Yeah. You could have given me a little warning though," she moaned.

"You're lucky I got you when I did." He yanked his cell phone out of his back pocket, speed dialed Brandon.

"We're under attack," he growled to Brandon.

"You're what?" Brandon exclaimed in disbelief.

"We're under attack," Liam repeated. "I thought you said this place was safe."

At that moment, the glass in the front door shattered and a small missile struck the bookcase two feet above Hayley's head. Both Liam and Hayley jerked, ducked closer to the floor.

Murdock commenced barking, charged the front door once more.

"Was that the front door or back door?" Brandon demanded.

"Front door," Liam answered.

"If you can escape from the back door, follow that sawmill road I told you about. There's an abandoned shack further in the woods. Be careful of the motion sensor light on the porch. Shoot it out if you have too. I'm sending reinforcements. One of the deputies in the town keeps an eye on the cabin for me."

"Make it fast," Liam ordered before he and Hayley crawled toward the door to the back porch. Liam handed Hayley the mini-LED flashlight he carried in his back pocket.

"I'm going to take out the security light, but you should have enough moonlight to make your way to the sawmill road. Once you're in the woods, you can use the flashlight. Keep going till you find the shack. Murdock and I will take care of these jerks, join you as soon as we can."

"Liam" Hayley started to object but Liam cupped the back of her neck, smothered her mouth with his.

"Now's not the time to argue, Red. Do it," he ordered as he opened the door, shot the security light before it could blink on.

He grabbed Brandon's baseball bat next to the door and turned to Murdock.

"Go get 'em," he told the dog who raced past him, around to the front of the cabin. His movement triggered the motion sensor lights on each corner, flooding the front of the cabin with a bright glare.

Liam nudged Hayley toward the road, followed the sounds of Murdock's growls, hoped the sudden brightness would blind the men long enough for him to make his way into the woods. He broke into a run when he saw Murdock lunge at the tall man, lock his jaws around the man's lower arm, caused him to drop the rifle. Liam swung the bat with all he had, whacked the guy across his shoulders upsetting his balance as he lunged forward, his head connecting with a tree trunk. He fell unconscious.

Liam checked for a pulse, looked up when he overheard Murdock attacking another interloper. Saw another closing in, his gun pointed at the dog, trying to aim for a good shot. Liam whistled, ordered Murdock to go help Hayley while he moved toward the two men, continually swinging the bat and shifting his position to make them readjust their fight plan. He lunged as if hitting a slider baseball and whacked the rifle out of the second guy's hand.

When a third one joined them, Liam delivered, short, vicious pokes with the bat at one of the men, broke away, paused, then engaged the other. Went on the offensive, concentrated on the third but delivered a foot kick into the groin of the middleman, sending him crashing against a tree, knocking him unconscious when his head jerked back.

Liam used his arms to control the distance between the two remaining trespassers, shoved them when they got too close. Twitching his hands and arms, he aimed at vulnerable points with clear knockout punches.

He tossed the bat aside, got one in a neck clinch, used him as a shield, kept kneeing the clinched guy to subdue his punches. Squeezed his elbows together to increase the lock on his head so he lost consciousness. Three down, still the one.

No sooner had the third one fallen; Liam was tackled by the fourth. He managed to roll away, jumped up to balance himself to fight the guy when out of nowhere a dirt bike roared past him.

The driver of the dirt bike punched the guy in the jaw, sent him down.

"Hayley's around back," Liam sprinted around to the backside of the cabin.

Hayley had made it to the edge of the woods before she picked up on the cracking sound of sticks leaves and brush being crushed. She turned toward the noise, surprised the intruder with a swift punch to his face. She snarled at the cracking sound of jaw and neck when his head jolted back. While he struggled to regain his balance, orient himself, she delivered a hard kick in the groin, cheered herself on when he leaned over and groaned.

But when she tried to deliver another kick to the side of his face, he grabbed her foot, yanked it up causing her to fall backwards.

She breathed a sigh of relief when she heard Murdock's growls as he charged her attacker from behind. The guy swung around, yelled out when Murdock locked his jaws around his lower arm. He tried to hit Murdock with his handgun but the dog's constant movement as he put all his furious agitated strength into yanking the man side to side made it too difficult.

Hayley jumped up, grabbed for a fallen log, gave the guy a swift whack on the side of his face. The guy put his free arm up, tried to fight her off, but with her supercharged adrenaline, Hayley hit at his arm and midsection until he fell to his knees. She gave him another whack on the back of his head, sent him face down to the ground. The anger was so intense, she began to cry as she continued to hit the man, blow after blow, splintering the log with each strike.

Liam raced over to grab the bloody log out of her hand. He tossed it aside, yanked her close. Wrapped his arms around her shaking body, tucked her sobbing face into the curve of his neck as he tried to calm her.

We can't stay here," Hayley announced as she glared at the six men who sat facing each other, next to the steps to the front porch. Their hands and feet were zip tied; a separate rope was tied around each of their ankles linking the six of them together. Several of the men would require medical attention for their bruised and swollen faces.

Convinced his truck was bugged for the thugs to have located them so quickly, Liam was searching the vehicle for a tracker.

Hayley sat on the front steps next to their dirt bike champion, the deputy Brandon had called in as backup. Dirk Browning was in his mid-twenties, had been with the Sheriff's department for five years. Tall, athletic, he'd been handy rounding up the unconscious criminals.

Dirk had just talked with the Sheriff who was arranging for a van to pick up the army of intruders.

Her face was puffy from her crying jag, but Hayley didn't care. She was safe and alive. That was what mattered. She studied the bruised and battered brute that had tried to kill her, amazed that she had lost control of her emotions.

"I guess our cover is blown," she breath a deep sigh. "We need to escape before more damage is done to Brandon's cabin. I feel so bad about what's been done already."

"A door can be replaced, the bullet hole patched," the Deputy commiserated. "You're safe and unharmed, that's what's most important. I know the guys that built the cabin, they can take care of that." Dirk chuckled. "Brandon won't be able to live this down for a while. You have a literal squad here trying to take you out. Mind sharing what did you did?"

"Long story," Hayley answered.

"Fuck," Liam yelled at that moment from beneath the truck.

Dirk nodded his head toward Liam. "Your friend doesn't sound so happy."

"No one was supposed to know we were here."

Liam crawled out from under the truck, walked over to join them. Hel held a small square black GPS tracking device in his hand.

"Found this on the inside of the back bumper. Only one place I could have picked this sucker up." He raised his hand, tossed it as hard as he could into the woods. "Guess that would explain the pale blue car this afternoon."

"I spotted two cars parked on the side of the road on my way here to the cabin. Must have hiked in. We can take care of them tomorrow."

"One of them should be blue with two black stripes on the passenger side. I noticed it yesterday before we left

Clippersville. Good chance whoever drove it murdered Sebastian Ortiz."

Everyone turned toward the lights of the Sheriff's car as it emerged from the wooded drive. It was followed by a van.

After introductions were made, the men loaded into the van, Liam looked at Hayley.

"Looks like we're on the move again, Red. We can't stay here."

"You're welcome to stay in town,"the Sheriff suggested.

"No but thank you." Hayley vetoed the suggestion. "I don't want to put anyone else in harm's way. I'm certain the town will have enough to talk about for the next month or so."

She started up the steps, paused midway. "Are you sure you can secure this place after we're gone? With the damaged door?"

"No problem," Dirk offered. "I'll be staying here till the repairs are done."

Brandon rubbed the back of his neck, gulped the coffee to keep him alert as he studied the footage of the prison's surveillance camera. The warden hadn't appreciated the late-night call but when he was informed of the attack on Hayley, had complied with the warning that he ran a shipshape prison.

His body tense, hands moving in jerks, fingers rapping against the desk, the sound of his pounding heart growing louder in his ears by the minute, Brandon hadn't appreciated Liam's implication there was a mole in his organization when he questioned the safety of the cabin.

He realized Liam spoke in the heat of the moment, but it irritated him that Liam should even question his loyalties at this stage in the game. They were friends and he hated the distrust. He was determined to prove his team was dependable with no moles, figured he'd start with Liam's visit to the prison.

Grinding his teeth, nostrils flaring, he cracked his knuckles as he concentrated on the file, sat up straight when he spied the guard moving toward Liam's truck.

Lips flatten. "Gotcha." He pounded the desk.

He grabbed his cell phone, speed dialed Liam.

"Someone at the prison is on the Ortiz payroll. Just watched him put the tracker on your truck. Will send someone to the prison now to discuss it with the warden."

Why hadn't anyone reported in? He bristled, leaned back in his chair, brushed his hands down his face in exhaustion. He'd sent an army in to get the job done, been up most of the night waiting, why hadn't he heard anything?

Walker and the bitch probably discovered by now he isn't dead. Now he'd be looking over his shoulder worrying if his cover had been blown.

It aggravated him the harder he worked at getting rid of the bitch, the closer they were getting to finding him.

He'd almost lost it when he learned they had visited Sebastian. Should have taken care of that problem sooner. Wondered what Sebastian told them. Would he have spilled his guts or played it cool. Hoped he'd ordered the hit in time.

They might know he's still alive, but he'd taken bought himself some time, he thought as he glared at himself in the mirror above the credenza. Studied his darkened hair, moustache and beard. Decided he liked the new image. Didn't care for the contacts that made his eyes a different color. He only wore them for important occasions. When he needed to mingle with the public.

They may have found his camera in Turner's office, but they still don't know about his prize link.

Chapter Eighteen

Liam settled in the chair on the back deck, brushed his hands down his face, tossed his head back to stare at the darkening skies. They'd been back in Vermont almost twenty-four hours and he was exhausted.

Much as he appreciated the quiet, he knew it wouldn't stay that way for long. Another hit was imminent, could occur any time.

He and Murdock had patrolled the property, checked the cameras. Now waited for the next invasion.

Hayley's breakdown after the attack at the cabin worried him. He understood her frustration, why she'd lost control, but he didn't want her doubting her strength. He'd stated they needed to train more and ordered her to the basement first thing that morning.

"I have my writing," she'd countered. "Mornings are my most creative times."

"Your training and safety are more important. You can write after we finish."

It also bothered him he hadn't informed Gerard Turner of the latest turn of events for fear the boss would pull him off the job. Which might be the solution, fluttered through his mind.

Now that he knew the house was safe, he'd recruit Brandon, or someone else to stay with Hayley and he'd go rogue. Search for Ortiz on his own. Might have better luck that way, wouldn't be worrying about Hayley all the time.

Yeah, right, he admonished himself. Like Red wasn't always on his mind.

His brows knitted when he thought about Brandon. Concerned about the change in their relationship. Regretted that he'd taken a dig at Brandon's organization.

Their last communication had been a short and clipped email from Brandon reporting the mole in the prison had been apprehended and relieved of his duties. Liam debated giving his friend a call.

Liam looked up when Hayley, with Murdock shadowing her in excitement, nudged the back door aside and plopped the dog's box of toys on the wood decking. He cringed when she reached inside, held the bright material up to his face.

"What's my favorite scarf doing in here?" she demanded, then yelped when she looked closer and discovered the sweatshirt she'd been missing for weeks.

"You're not the only one that needs training," Liam defended the dog.

Hayley grabbed the familiar notebook, gave Liam the evil eye.

"This is my thinking notebook." She leafed through the pages that were wrinkled from being wet, the ink smeared. "What good is this going to do me now?"

"I'd intended to put it back, but it rained before he could track it, so I had to keep it hidden. Guess I should have buried it," he tried to joke.

Hayley leafed through the pages, figured she should be able to read most of the weepy clues, remember what she'd been thinking. She shook her head when she discovered one of her hair clips, then cried out when she spied the single earring in the corner of the box.

"My earrings?" she turned on him. "You hid one of my favorite earrings?" she rested the long loop in the palm of her hand.

"I have to keep challenging him," Liam shrugged a shoulder. His eyes strayed to the necklace around her neck, raised his hands in the air when Hayley saw the look and covered the necklace with a hand.

"Don't even think about it," she ordered.

"I wouldn't. I know how much it means to you. That's why I chose the earring, I wanted to see if Murdock could track you with something so small."

Liam glanced down at the dog who sat beside him, rubbed his head between his ears. "This was before the last attack and I must have tossed it in the box, forgot about it."

Hayley stared into the woods outside the window of her office. Hard as she tried to focus on the manuscript, she worried when the next blow would come.

Her writing was suffering, Faith and Kyle were arguing all the time, the plot seemed to be falling apart. She can't focus for thinking about the army that attacked them at the cabin. Worried another would come to the house.

Her eyes blinked when inspiration for the story flickered through her thoughts. She grabbed some scrap paper, began making notes.

What if the culprits in her mystery were a cartel and the victim was in the wrong place at the wrong time? Murdered because she happened to witness a drug transaction or transfer of women being trafficked.

She straightened, began to squiggle in her chair while the ideas flowed.

What if Faith and Kyle decide to go back to the scene of the crime, visit the neighborhood. Eyeball members of the cartel watching them from across the street.

What if Faith and Kyle decide to stake out the neighborhood, are ambushed and Kyle saves Faith's life. Sits at her bedside all night in the hospital. Confesses why he became a cop.

When her hand couldn't keep up with her thoughts, Hayley turned to her laptop and started dictating, followed Kyle's backstory as it evolved with his dialog.

"When I was in college, one of my best friends was raped and beaten on the campus. I stayed with her in the hospital, realized the identity of her rapist when she rambled during her sleep, awoke, and talked to me. I started following the guy. Turned out he had a drug habit and decided to break into the house of this rich old man that lived down the street from where he lived. I followed him and when he beat the man and was rummaging through the house, I managed to sneak into the house. I attacked him from behind, beat the shit out of the guy. Left him with the old man at the scene, made an anonymous nine-one-one call on my way home. Unfortunately, the old man died, but the guy never knew who attacked him. He's still in prison and I've managed to sit in on all his parole hearings."

It dawned on Hayley her two protagonists were falling in love. Like she had fallen in love with Liam. She inhaled a deep breath, appreciative that her story was back on track. All she needed to do was help Faith and Kyle prove the gang had killed the victim.

Plotting and describing Kyle's emotions for Faith, helped Hayley to understand Liam's dedication to protecting her. Yes, he was doing his job, but she needed to show her appreciation, make it up to him. She smiled as her imagination once again kicked into overdrive.

She started with the meal. Suggested since it was supposed to be a nice cool evening, they enjoy their dinner outside. He'd grill the steaks, she'd handle the salad, prepare the potatoes and asparagus for roasting alongside the steaks.

Then she changed into the outfit he'd bought her in Boston.

After the meal, they finished off the bottle of wine on the deck.

"Liam, I know I can be a pain, sometimes, but I hope you know how much I appreciate your being here."

"Part of the job," he shrugged, "but I must admit there's never a dull moment with you, Red. And I'm not talking about the break-ins. You have a way of keeping things lively."

"Are you saying I have charm?" She toyed with a lock of her hair.

Liam studied the gleam in her eyes, realized she was flirting with him. Should have suspected it sooner when she'd changed into that outfit, brought back memories of the first time they'd been together. Decided maybe this was the release they needed. He was tired of always bickering and arguing with her. Worrying about what would happen next.

Hayley felt breathless, nervous that her seduction might be working.

"How's the book coming? Are your protagonists getting along?" Liam queried.

"Great. In fact, Faith, that's my female detective, has realized she's falling in love with Kyle, the rich kid partner. He saved her from being assaulted, sat by her bed all night in the hospital. She wants to make it up to him and I'm working on the seduction scene."

"Seduction, huh. You don't have too much of that in your books. More murder and mayhem, bloody fights and vicious killings."

"Yeah, I realized I needed some practice with the seduction." She smiled; things were going as planned.

"Need some ideas," he joked.

"No," she set her glass on the table, "just a guinea pig."

Liam's heart thumped at her brazenness, decided he might enjoy seeing how far she'd go. "I'm all yours," he offered.

"You sure?" She stood slowly, stepped over to straddle him, rested her arms atop his shoulders, her forehead against his.

Warmth spread through her, and her heart skipped when he rested his hands on either side of her hips. She brushed her lips against his, moved to his cheek.

"Don't want to force you to do something you wouldn't want to do," she whispered in his ear before she nibbled his earlobe.

Liam swallowed, as heat coursed through his veins. Felt his body coming alive. More so when she reached for the hem of her blouse, pulled it over her head. He stared at the exquisite necklace that rested between her naked breasts.

"Red," his mouth edged up in a half smile, "You never cease to amaze me."

He took hungry possession of her mouth, his probing tongue probed sipped the wine, elicited a moan when his hands eased up her sides, cupped and kneaded her breasts, his thumbs dancing over her throbbing nipples. He angled her head to deepen the kiss.

Heat curled down Hayley's spine as she pressed her warm center against his iron-hard arousal and shimmied back and forth.

His lips still locked on her, Liam cupped her bottom and stood. "We need to take this inside, Red." He mumbled against Hayley's smiling lips as her legs tightened around his waist, her arms around his neck.

Thinking he planned to carry her upstairs to the bedroom, Hayley was surprised to find herself deposited on the table in thc dining area of the kitchen. She gaped when he quickly locked the door, stepped out of his jeans and yanked hers away with two quick gestures.

He leaned over her, his mouth covered was on hers, inhaled the screams of orgasm that swamped her as he hammered her on the sturdy oak table.

The *motion detected* alert on Liam's phone awakened them hours later. Murdock was already pacing as Liam studied the movement at the front door. Angry that the cameras hadn't picked up their activity earlier.

"Must have marched right up the drive," he complained as he yanked on his jeans. "Get to the stairwell and call nine-one-one," he ordered when he overheard the jimmying at the front door.

"Liam, let me help."

"You watch from the stairwell. Let Murdock and me do our jobs."

Hayley grabbed her sweats and shoes, dressed while she studied the screens on the stairwell walls.

Her stomach tightened with worry while Liam waited at the bottom of the steps. Then she drew a deep breath when he tackled the lead guy as he moved into the living room. Her muscles tensed when she saw a second guy charge, but Liam must have been aware of him because he leaped up, dodged the guy's punch with two fingers to the guy's eyes. Murdock took over and locked his jaws around the blinded man's lower arm.

Suddenly Hayley caught movement at the back door, watched the door slide and another man snuck inside, planning to sneak up behind Liam.

She grabbed the Glock off the wall, dashed down the stairs, exited through the door into the pantry. She cracked the pantry door open, peeked around the corner to see the man hesitate at the opening between the kitchen and living room and aim his gun at Liam.

Hayley raised her own gun, aimed it at the guy.

"Hey," she shouted, before shooting at his foot. He yelled out in pain, turned to aim at her but she gave him another round in the stomach. When he collapsed on the floor, she raced over and hit his head with the butt of the gun.

Hayley jolted when Murdock yelped and looked over to see the blinded guy manage to toss her dog against the wall, winding him. Murdock lay still on the floor. Upset that her dog is wounded, Hayley rushed into the room, aimed for the guy's knee and fired.

Liam was able to deliver a blow to his assailant's midsection, then his chin when the guy looked over in surprise to see his partner in crime collapse.

When the first guy hobbled toward Hayley, she backed up and when he continued to advance, she shot his other knee.

"Do you want me to kill you," she screamed when he began to move again. Hayley felt the adrenaline building and began to visibly shake. "Because I'll do it," she lunged at him.

Liam raced over, managed to get the gun out of Hayley's hand.

"Red," he wrapped an arm around her shoulder, tried to calm her. "It's okay. It's okay," he repeated as he kissed the top of her head. "Go open the front gate. The Sheriff should be getting here any minute."

Hayley stared at him in a daze, realized she'd shot two men, not once but twice. She worried what she would do the next time.

The following day, Hayley, Liam, Brandon and Sheriff Collins sat around the table discussing their next move.

Hayley set Liam's coffee in front of him and couldn't help but remember what had happened the previous night in that very spot.

"I refuse to go to a safehouse," Hayley vetoed Liam's suggestion moments later. "I want this nightmare to end, and I don't see how a safehouse is going to do so."

Brandon nodded in agreement. "All you'd be doing is putting if off. Whoever is doing this, Simon Ortiz or whomever, they will figure it out and start another search."

"You're not telling me something I haven't already told myself," Liam retaliated. "I've even considered pulling myself off the case. Go after the guy myself. Maybe I'm too close to the case, too involved. Let new eyes look at things."

"You don't want to split the team," Jack Collins stated. "You've got eyes in all the right places; you just need to rule out the suspects."

"Someone has turned the plant in the boss's office. Must have happened during the attack at the cabin. So that means they are still watching him. I'm checking the backups for any visuals."

"What about the Assistant, Katherine Jenkins?" Liam asked. "Did you ever find out anything more on her husband's killing?"

Brandon shook his head. "The local police say they've hit a dead end and moved on to more important cases." When Jack Collins frowned, Brandon went on to explain. "The Assistant's husband went hunting last December in Erie County, New York and didn't come home. Ms. Jenkins reported him missing and they found him dead in the woods two days later. They said it wasn't a suicide, but no one has come forward to report any hunting mishaps either."

"Erie County? That's my home territory," Jack mused. "What you're telling me sounds a little too suspicious. I can follow up with some friends in the area and get some answers. What worries me is that may have been arranged as well."

"Then we'll arrange a meeting with Katherine Jenkins," Liam decided.

"I suggest you stay outside the city," Brandon offered. "Just pick a spot and stop. There are too many eyes and ears everywhere. We can keep in touch via cell phones. Interview Katherine Jenkins at Florence's office. Come up with an excuse to get her there."

On his way out the door, Jack Collins turned to Hayley, cupped his hands around her upper arms.

"Liam told me you took it hard about shooting those men last night."

"Yes, sir. I feel like my life and emotions are spiraling out of control. I've never shot anyone and worry I'll kill someone before it's over."

"I don't want you to hesitate the next time you're in a situation like that. Just remember, these people are after you and won't hesitate to kill you. You do what you need to do to protect yourself and if that means killing someone, then that's what you do. It's called self-defense."

Chapter Nineteen

Florence Sunden studied the blonde who stepped into the office ahead of Liam Walker and Brandon Anderson.

"You can take that wig off missy," she commented with her Yonkers accent.

Liam jerked; Brandon's face broke into a bright smile.

"This is Amelia Cox," Liam introduced Hayley to Florence.

"I'm well acquainted with her." Florence stood, fisted tiny hands on her tiny waist. "And she doesn't have to hide her identity from me. I used to bounce her on my knee when she was a little girl."

Hayley laughed out loud, rushed around the counter to give the short woman a hug.

"How are you, Grandma? I've missed you so much."

Hayley's real grandparents had died before she was born, so Florence had become her honorary substitute. She'd worked side by side with her mother, often babysat Hayley when Gerard and Julia Turner attended fundraisers. They had comforted one another after Julia Turner was killed.

It had also comforted Hayley to know that Florence was her contact with Savannah Hughes and coordinated all the packages she received from her publishers. Florence was one of the major people Hayley had missed during her seclusion despite the notes she often slipped a note inside her packages. Hayley had missed that Yonkers accent, the friendly banter.

"And I've missed you." Florence cast adoring eyes up at Hayley. "Told your daddy the other day he needed to take better care of you. Bring you home before I'm six feet under."

Liam studied the two women who were as different as night and day. One was tall, slender with vivid auburn hair, the other short and chunky, cropped snow-white hair. Both had tears in their eyes.

He had met Florence three times since he began working for Gerard Turner, mainly talked to her over the phone. He had no idea Florence had been so prominent in Hayley's life or was aware of her alias.

Florence chuckled at Liam confusion. "It was before your time, sonny, but back in the day, in my younger years I was more involved in Gerard Turner's office. Became Julia's second hand. She would bring Hayley by the office."

"I always looked forward to your suckers or treats." Hayley rested her cheek on the top of Florence's head, smiled at Liam. "Another reason I shared treats with Zoe."

"Okay," Florence gave Hayley a quick before rubbing her small hands together. "I understand we need to schedule a meeting."

Katherine Jenkins studied the email that popped up on her screen.

"Just received an important package for Mr. Turner marked top priority. Wondered if you could stop by to sign for it. Not certain if he needs it for his meetings on the

West Coast. I would bring it to you myself, but I've been swamped here with work. I will be here until four this afternoon."

Katherine smiled. She was a tall, full-figured woman with soft manicured hands that were used to skimming the keyboard, scheduling appointments, taking notes during intense board meetings. She was also a proud woman. Took pride in working for Gerard Turner and her professional appearance, keeping her salt and pepper hair styled into a classic French twist, oval face with soft creamy skin, immaculately groomed, arched eyebrows over hazel eyes plucked and neat.

She always dressed in two-piece suits but since her boss was out of town, she'd opted for the casual guise with cashmere pants, white blouse but kept it professional with the pearl necklace around her neck, earrings on her dainty ears.

She'd been Gerard Turner's Executive Assistant for almost five years now, having replaced Grace Walker after her unfortunate death. She often chatted with Florence Sunden who had been a wonderful mentor for her while she'd adjusted to working with the busy tycoon.

Florence had also been a friend after the death of her husband last December.

With Mr. Turner out of the office, Katherine had debated leaving a little early and decided maybe she'd just use this as her excuse to get out of the office.

"I can be there by three thirty," she typed her response. *"It will be good to visit with you some."*

"She took the bait," Florence announced to her room full of occupants. Hayley and Murdock sat off to the side, Liam and Brandon paced while awaiting the reply.

"Gives us an hour to prepare," Brandon rubbed his hands together.

When Gerard Turner had been called to the West Coast late yesterday for an emergency meeting, Liam and Brandon jumped into action. Realized this was their opportunity to interview the Assistant without alerting the boss. It was evident they couldn't meet in the office because it was being surveilled or call her because her phone was wiretapped.

The only reasonable alternate site was Florence's office. It was away from the head office, and no one would suspect her stopping by the shipping office to pick up a package for her boss. Or having an impromptu chat in Florence's small back room which was out of public view.

It served as Florence's sorting room, but Hayley decided the simple square table and four chairs reminded her of the interview room in her book minus the observation mirror.

Katherine Jenkins arrived promptly at half past three that afternoon. She strolled into the office and stepped around the front counter to greet Flo with a hug. Jumped when the back-room door opened behind her.

"Oh, Brandon," Katherine exclaimed when he wandered out of the room. "I didn't expect to see you here. I thought you were out of town; might be with Mr. Turner."

Brandon offered a bright friendly smile. "I had some correspondence to take care of but am glad I caught you here. I need to have a word with you. Do you mind if we step in here for a minute?"

Katherine frowned, nibbled on her bottom lip, twisted the hand on the shoulder strap of her purse. Was reminded of her younger days when she'd feared being summoned to the principal's office and wracked her brain, wondering if she might have done something wrong.

"Of course," she answered. She blinked when she found the small meeting room occupied by Liam Walker, a woman with long blonde hair and a tall dog.

Katherine offered her hand to Liam.

"Mr. Walker, I had no idea you were in town either. It's so nice to see you."

Liam smiled, gave her a brief hug as he wanted to keep her at ease. He turned to Hayley.

"This is Amelia Cox."

Liam wanted to gauge Katherine's reaction, saw no recognition as the two women shook hands. Katherine would have started working for Gerard Turner after Grace was killed. She might not be aware of Hayley's existence since Hayley was in the hospital at the time, then disappeared.

He'd always wondered if Gerard Turner ever mentioned Hayley to his Assistant. Realized he hadn't.

Brandon pulled the chair out for Katherine. Offered to get her some water which she declined.

"I apologize for being so secretive with this, but Liam and I have been working a sensitive case and we wanted to talk with you away from the office. And to put your mind at ease, Mr. Turner will be informed of this meeting."

"Ms. Jenkins, have you had anyone calling or stopping by the office in recent weeks?" Liam started the questioning.

Katherine leaned back in her seat, considered the question. "No more than usual. Mr. Turner is a busy man; we have people in and out the office all the time."

"But no one out of the ordinary?" Liam persisted.

Katherine frowned, nodded her head. Wondered if maybe she should have been more observant.

"No, no one out of the ordinary."

Brandon leaned forward, linked his fingers on the table as he debated how to best broach his question. "Ma'am, I know you're recently widowed but have you been seeing anyone?"

Katherine slid him a guarded look, taken aback that he would be asking about her private life.

"Brandon, I loved my husband, and his death was such a shock. It upsets me that those people haven't found the person who killed him. I have no desire to see anyone else. And even if I did, there is so little time with Mr. Turner being so busy." She paused when a face popped into her head. "Except"

"Except?" Liam sat upright on alert.

Katherine shrugged a shoulder, her cheeks turned pink.

"Well, there is this one man." She began to wring her hands in her lap worried she might have done something wrong.

"A man," Liam prompted.

"Yes, James. James Simon." She squirmed in her chair. "I met him at one of Mr. Turner's fundraisers. He's another generous donor. I don't think Mr. Turner is acquainted with him but he's been to several recent events. He sent me some flowers a few weeks back."

Liam, Hayley and Brandon exchanged expressions at the coincidence of the name. All three were certain the *James Simon* Katherine Jenkins had mentioned was Simon Ortiz.

"How well do you know him?" Brandon murmured, tried to ease her nerves. "Have you seen much of him lately?"

Hayley reached for her cell phone, scrolled through her photos for the picture she took of Simon Ortiz from the newspaper article.

"Ms. Jenkins," Hayley offered her phone to her father's Assistant, "does this man resemble James Simon?"

Katherine jumped when Hayley spoke, she'd been so quiet from the beginning. She leaned forward to study the picture.

"It's a little fuzzy but yes, it could be James Simon. The man I've met has a moustache and beard."

Hayley, Liam and Brandon once again exchanged relieved expressions.

"What can you tell us about him?" Liam inquired.

"Nothing much. He seems a friendly sort. Always pleasant to talk to." She shifted as her cheeks became rosier. "He asked me out a few weeks ago but I was unable to go. It's just too soon if you know what I mean."

"Has he contacted you in the past week?"

Katherine thought a minute. "I never take personal calls, but he did call the office the other day. Asked if he could have a quick meeting with Mr. Turner but that was the day he was out of town."

"The day he was in Boston?" Liam prompted.

"Yes. I told him he was out of town for the afternoon but would be at the fundraiser that evening if he wanted to talk to him then."

"Did you tell him he was in Boston?"

"No," Katherine frowned. "Or course not. In fact, I didn't find out Mr. Turner had gone to Boston until the next day."

"Okay," Brandon assured her. "Like I said, we've been having some security issues and Liam and I are going to check on this James Simon. We have reason to believe he is a very dangerous man."

"Oh my," Brandon paused when Katherine became visibly upset, covered her lips with red tipped fingers. "But he seemed so charming. So sincere."

"They always are," Liam muttered.

"Ms. Jenkins," Brandon continued, "Earlier this week I did a sweep of the office and discovered your telephone and desk have been bugged. There is also a camera in the boss's office. Someone is tracking your calls and the activity in Mr. Turner's office. We have reason to believe James Simon is behind it and I encourage you to not have any more dealings with him. We're not going to remove the bug; we don't want to alert whoever it is that we're on to them. But it would be best if you are more careful what you say and start taking notes. In the meantime, if you think of anything or if something should come up, please send me an email."

Liam navigated the truck toward the interstate back to the hotel. It was dusk.

Florence had turned the *Closed* sign on the door, decided to take Katherine out for an early dinner to calm the Assistant's nerves.

Liam, Hayley and Brandon had stayed in the office discussed what to do next. Brandon would assign someone to do a background search of this James Simon locate his whereabouts. Liam and Hayley would lay low.

"I can't believe Simon Ortiz has been able to masquerade around as James Simon and no one has recognized him," Hayley fumed. "Or that he has been so close to my father."

"We'll get him," Liam consoled her as he stopped for the light. "Now we have proof who we're dealing with, we can focus on finding him. Brandon can put out feelers, start tracking his whereabouts. If he's as generous a donor as Katherine Jenkins says he is, he must have contacts, connections in the city."

Hayley breathed a sigh of relief; thought about the possibility that her days of anonymity were almost over. All they needed to do was track the monster, tie him to the attempts on her life, convict him. Then she would be free of the pain and frustration. And Liam who would no longer have to safeguard her.

Her heart skipped when she realized he would no longer have a reason to be in her life. What would he do? Move on to another job?

What would it be like to not have him around, getting in her way, irritating her. Hounding her to take care of herself.

She turned to study his sharp profile as he started through the intersection. Her glistening, tear-filled eyes grew round when she stared at the bright lights of an oncoming vehicle approaching full speed toward Liam's side of the truck.

There was a sudden loud crash as the truck jolted from the collision, skidded twenty yards to the right onto a side street of the intersection and Hayley's world turned black.

Chapter Twenty

Liam was floating but sinking fast. He jerked as he began to awaken, swim for the surface. Everything was black and he ached all over. He tried to reposition himself, felt like he'd been hit by a freight train.

He detected a beeping noise that became erratic, realized it matched his heart's rapid beat as it blared in his throbbing head.

Pictures of Hayley, conversations with Brandon, Gerard Turner, Katherine Jenkins and Florence Sunden flashed through his head as he bobbed, drifted in the darkness. Out of the blue, there were bright lights and an explosion as he was jolted awake, grabbed the bed's siderails to steady himself.

Liam opened his eyes, squeezed them shut when the bright florescent light over the bed glared back at him. He scrunched them until his eyes adjusted, took in the white ceiling tiles, pale ivory walls. He distinguished what had to be an orchestra of muffled voices, cries of pain, beeping of other machines competing with the nagging dings of the machine next to his bed.

He surveyed the myriad of aches and pains jolting throughout his body. Besides his throbbing head, his neck was stiff and left shoulder pounded like someone had taken a jackhammer to it. His stomach was nauseous; and he felt like shit.

He fought the grogginess but knew something was different about his left arm, winced when he peered down, found it was bandaged. He tried to focus on the blurry shadow near the end of the bed, realized it was a nurse noting his vitals on those roaming computers they were always pushing.

"Where's Hayley?" He demanded.

The nurse jumped in reaction.

"Hayley?"

"Yeah, the woman that was with me."

"Sir, you were the only patient brought in."

"What do you mean?" His eyes expanded as he tried to sit up, fell back when the dizziness hit him.

Liam heard footsteps, looked over to see Brandon rush past the window that separated the small room from the nurse's station and hub of the emergency room.

"Where's Hayley?" Liam badgered his friend, his eyes dilated and anxious. "Is she with you?"

Brandon raised his hand to quieten Liam, turned a bright smile on the nurse. "Could you give us a minute?"

"A minute," the nurse warned. "The doctor wants him on some pain medication."

"I don't need any pain medication. I want to get the hell out of here," Liam barked from the narrow bed. "Brandon, tell me, where Hayley is."

Brandon nudged the nurse out the door, closed it.

"She wasn't with you."

Both men stared at the heart monitor that began dinging while the pressure cuff around Liam's upper arm clicked on, started tightening. Liam clenched his jaw, tried to calm himself while the pressure cuff did its business.

Knew he'd have to gain control of his frayed nerves before anyone would release him from the hospital.

"You know she was. So was Murdock. "Liam jolted. "Where's he? Was he hurt?"

"Murdock's fine. Gave the paramedics a fit when they tried to pull you out of the wreckage. Good thing you put my number on his dog tag. The police on the scene called me, that's how I found about the accident."

"What about Hayley?"

"Hayley wasn't with you when the police arrived on the scene. I just talked to the paramedics; they confirmed you were the only occupant in the truck. What happened?"

Liam stared through the blinds of the window. "We were on our way back to the room, waiting at this intersection. Talking about how we needed to be patient, it wouldn't be long before the nightmare was over. The light changed, she smiled at me then her eyes grew round and out of the blue I was t-boned. This vehicle appeared out of nowhere.

"One minute Hayley was talking to me and the next, there was this jolt on my left, my airbag opened, the truck was sliding. Must have knocked us both unconscious. You're sure she's not here?"

Brandon nodded his head.

Liam grabbed for his cell phone, realized he wasn't dressed. He was in a hospital gown in a narrow bed, the side rails up.

"Where's my phone? I need my phone."

Brandon turned, began searching the room, located the torn jeans and tattered shirt tossed on the floor in the corner on the other side of the bed. He frisked the pockets, located Liam's cell phone.

Liam grabbed it, checked his apps. Breathed a sigh of relief when he eyeballed the blinking blue dot.

"You've got to get me out of here."

"Liam, you've been injured, the paramedics mentioned you might have a concussion. You heard the nurse; the doctor wants you on some pain meds."

"I don't give a shit about pain meds. We've got to find Hayley before it's too late. She may be wandering the city in a daze, or Ortiz has her." He unwrapped the pressure cuff when it started the process again. Tossed it across the room.

"What time is it? How long have I been here? I need some clothes. Help me out of here," Liam rattled off.

"It's going on seven," Brandon checked his wristwatch, yanked his cell phone out of his back pocket. "I'm not sure you're ready for release but give me a minute" He pressed Liam against the mattress. "Maybe Florence can help us out."

"There's my boy," Florence gushed as she rushed into the room thirty minutes later. Her eyes brimming with tears, she pressed a bag against Brandon's chest as she raced to the narrow bed, planted a loud sloppy kiss on Liam's cheek.

She winked at Liam before she turned to the nurse, "I hope you've been taking excellent care of my grandson. I don't know what I'd do if anything were to happen to him."

Florence strolled over to the nurse, linked arms, guided her out into the hub of activity. "Now, I want you to help me locate the doctor that's been treating my only grandchild."

Brandon shook his head as the corners of his mouth turned up when he closed the door behind the women, pulled the cord to shut the blinds in the window.

Liam lowered the bed rail, sat upright to jump out of the bed, grabbed hold of the rails when his head spun. Took a moment to steady himself while Brandon emptied the contents of the bag onto the bed. Helped Liam change into the new jeans and shirt.

"I owe Florence big time," Liam groaned while Brandon slipped his loafers on his bare feet.

"You need to sit a minute," Brandon advised, "let your body balance itself."

But Liam was impatient. Time was of the essence. He needed to find Hayley. Didn't know whether Ortiz had her or what he'd do if he did. Would he string her along, make her suffer or just shoot her to get it over with?

Ten minutes later, Brandon cracked the door open, located Florence chatting with the nurses at the nurses' station. She watched both men leave then handed a business card to the nurse assigned to Liam.

"I appreciate you taking such wonderful care of my grandson. I'll give you a break and go sit with him for a while."

Florence made the pretense of entering Liam's room, shut the door behind her, gave it a few minutes, then snuck out of the hospital herself. Figured the nurse would be giving her a call soon enough about her grandson that had absconded the emergency room.

Brandon helped Liam into the truck where he was greeted by an excited Murdock. Liam winced when he reached back to reassure the dog.

"I want to go back to the scene," Liam ordered.

"It's late. Probably no one there."

Liam checked his phone. "Eight o'clock. You think after the excitement of our accident, no business isn't still open trying to make up for lost time?"

Brandon shrugged a shoulder. "Possible, but are you up to it?"

"I don't have a choice," Liam threw his head back against the seat. "Hayley's missing and until I find her, there's nothing else I can do."

They drove back to the scene of the accident. Traffic was light, most of the buildings were dark. Remnants of shattered glass sparkled beneath the streetlights.

Liam eased out of the truck, tucked his bandaged arm next to his stomach as he walked to the corner of the intersection. It was a narrow side street that crossed over the major thoroughfare of the city. He studied the rundown buildings. Not the best part of town. A pawn shop was located on one corner, catty corner from a convenience store, liquor store and vacant building the other two corners.

He looked up, searched for cameras. There was the usual monitor at the light, but it was aimed on the principal street, not the side street. The businesses might have interior cameras, but it was too dark to locate any outside security cameras.

Liam studied the buildings.

A lone figure stood outside the liquor store, hands and face pressed to the dark windows no doubt sorry the waterhole was closed. He turned and stumbled across the street to the convenience store.

Liam caught sight of movement in the tinted windows of the *Freedom Pawn Shop*, decided it would be worth checking. He and Brandon wandered over, decided to give the store some business.

Liam followed Brandon, winced at the bright florescent lights; his stomach gagged at the greasy, musty air. It was an extensive room crammed packed with TVs, radios, microwaves, toaster ovens, hard drives, laptops, musical instruments anything desperate people in a pinch for money relinquished. The local news broadcasted from the flat screen TV mounted above the glass top counter displaying pocket watches, wristwatches, rings, small collectibles and coins.

Considering Liam's condition, Brandon initiated the conversation.

"Understand you had some excitement outside earlier this evening."

"You could say that" the stocky man with military style hair cut studied them through narrowed eyes. He gave Liam a closer look when he heeded the bandage on his left arm. "If I didn't know better, I'd say you were in the accident."

"Yes, sir, I was," Liam answered. "Blindsided. The other vehicle came out of nowhere. My girlfriend was with me, but she's gone missing. You wouldn't by any chance have any security visuals of the accident, would you?"

"As a matter of fact, I was just looking at it before I set the cameras to close."

Liam jerked. "You haven't erased it, have you?"

"No."

"Do you mind if we see it?" Brandon asked. "We're trying to determine what happened to his girlfriend."

"The camera doesn't show too much of the accident, but it happened right there," he pointed a finger toward the door that opened to the street, "right outside my shop. I happened to look up when I overheard the noise of the collision. Saw the other truck ram yours, some guy jumped out, raced around to the passenger side. Threw the red head over his shoulder carried her to his truck. Your dog was trapped inside the truck, but he put up a major fuss when they guy took the woman."

The man studied Brandon. "I believe the police gave the dog to you."

"Yes, sir," Brandon agreed. "But when I talked to the police and the paramedics, they never said anything about the woman. We appreciate your being so observant."

The man shrugged a shoulder. "Didn't know whether she was a fugitive, or if it was a domestic dispute. The cops never asked."

"Had you ever seen the other truck or man before?" Brandon inquired.

The owner shook his head.

Liam grimaced as he reached for his wallet, struggled to remove a business card which he handed to the shop owner.

"That accident was intentional, and the woman is in grave danger. If you should remember anything or see either the truck or man again, I'd appreciate it if you'd give me a call. Thank you for your help."

Brandon and Liam turned to exit the building when Liam's cell phone chimed.

Chapter Twenty-One

Hayley shuddered in the darkness that clouded her subconscious. She grimaced at the sudden pain that shot through her head and across her shoulders when the echo of the loud boom of the hood of the oncoming truck crashing into Liam's side of the pickup jolted her awake. She recalled the seatbelt snapping taut as she was tossed to the side, then the instant pain and dizziness as her head bashed against the door.

Numb with shock, time become a series of flashes – the bright lights of the oncoming truck, Liam smiling at her, Grandma's laughter before their meeting with Katherine Jenkins, Murdock's warning yelp. Hayley inhaled a panicked fast breath as she jerked awake.

She lay on her side, disoriented about what had happened, where she was. The pain on her right side kicked in followed by a fluttering in her stomach and tightening in her chest when she thought about Liam, worried what had happened to him.

How long had she been here? Where was Liam?

She raised her hand to rub her aching forehead, only to realize both hands were tied together by sturdy nylon zip ties. She groaned; would she ever be free of those things.

Her hands lowered to her chest, and she breathed a sigh of relief when her fingers skimmed over the necklace, thankful that nothing had happened to it. She cradled the pendant between her fingers, sought the solace and determination she needed to get through whatever situation she was in. She would be strong, figure a way out of this ordeal. Outwit whoever had kidnapped her and escape to find Liam.

She focused on her breathing inhaled through her nose, exhaled through her mouth, intent on calming herself, making her muscles relax, free her mind of fear. Visualized where she wanted to be – out of this dark room.

With Liam.

She tried to recall everything that happened. Once again, she experienced the loud boom of the collision, tires screeching, brakes grinding and glass shattering. Relived the jerk of the seatbelt against her chest, pressing her back in the seat seconds before the impact and banging her head on the side window.

She remembered the door being yanked open, the fear of seeing the big hand and bigger knife, worrying if her demise was imminent. Experienced the release when the knife cut through the fabric of the seatbelt. She'd been disoriented, when those big hand pulled her from the wreck; suddenly she was weightless, must have passed out as her world went black.

Hayley winced when she turned to lay on her back, sensitive to the throbbing pull at the base of her neck and across her shoulders. Her eyes still closed, she let the dizziness pass so she could get her bearings.

It was so quiet, she hesitated to open her eyes, wondered if the shock had ruptured her eardrum. She worried if she did open her eyes, she would find some madman facing her, waiting for her to awaken so he could strangle her, watch her die.

When she gave in and peeked through narrowed eyes, she discovered she was in a darkened room.

She peered over to her right, scrutinized the lights that outlined a door. It appeared she was stowed away in a darkened room, her captor or captors in a connecting room. As her eyes adjusted, she detected what might be a dresser, assumed she was in a bedroom as she perceived the soft mattress of a bed beneath her.

Hayley couldn't restrain the smile that tugged at her lips. She was thankful her hands and feet weren't tied to the four corners of a bed like the victim in one of her books.

The quietness worried her. Was someone on the other side of that door or had she been dumped in an abandoned building to die from thirst and hunger?

She tugged at the zip tie, knew she needed to free herself if she was going to escape this place. She moaned as she struggled to sit upright, rested her elbows on her knees to gain her equilibrium, ease the dizziness. Realized her right shoulder and hip would be black and blue if they weren't already.

She gripped the end of the cord between her teeth to tightened it, then fought the pain in her upper arms and across her shoulders as she raised her hands above her head, put all her effort into lowering them against her stomach to break the tie. Leaned forward to rest her head in her hands when she succeeded.

Next, she reached down to jimmy the lock on her ankles.

She tugged her cell phone from her back pocket, thankful her captor hadn't thought to take it. Her battery registered thirty percent, but she was desperate to contact Liam. Needed to make sure he was okay.

Hayley speed-dialed Liam's number but before he can answer, she caught the sound of a footstep outside the door, jumped when the shadows moved across the bottom of the door.

She reached out, brushed a hand across the nightstand beside the bed, set the phone on the floor between the bed and the small table. Hoped it was out of sight of her captor.

Prayed he wouldn't hear Liam's voice should Liam answer.

Hayley didn't want to alert her captor that she had freed herself and managed to lay back on the bed as the doorknob turned. She had tucked her hands between her legs, bent her legs at the knees and tucked the balls of her feet against her bottom by the time her captor entered, flipped the light switch to cast the room into brightness.

"Where am I?" Hayley snarled loud enough for Liam to overhear should he answer her call. Hoped the sudden noise would startle her captor while her eyes adjusted to the light and she studied the room, gauged the size and strength of the unfamiliar man who held her captive.

"Your final resting place," a gruff voice answered just as loud. "Lucky for you the boss doesn't want you messed up like the other woman."

Hayley cast narrowed eyes on the stocky man she assumed had killed Savannah.

"You killed Savannah?"

He gave her a broad smile then flexed his hand. "My hand's still tender from the beating."

"Why did you have to kill her?"

"She was our link to you. Wouldn't talk. All she did was sob."

"Why me? Why am I here?"

"Let's just say your luck has run out."

"What happened to Liam?"

"Dead, I hope. Last I saw, he was slumped over the wheel. Bastard took out every one of my guys."

"I took out several myself," Hayley couldn't resist bragging. She flinched when the man raised his hand as if to backhand her.

"All the trouble you caused, I ought to get a few licks in before the boss gets here. At least I got the job done. Got him off my back for a while."

"Is that how you get your kicks? Beating on defenseless women?"

"It's what I do best," he gave her a broad smile.

Hayley's hatred increased as she studied the man through narrowed eyes. He was stocky, barrel chested with muscular arms and big hands. He had a square face, few days growth of beard, cold onyx eyes, lines across his forehead on either side of his mouth and a crooked nose that looked like it had been broken a couple times. She stared at his big hands, wide palms. Felt her fury as she imagined him beating her friend.

She tightened her muscles as she wanted so badly to jump up, take down the man that had killed Savannah. Realized she needed to wait. Discover who was the brains behind all the attacks.

"Who's your boss? The one pulling your strings." She egged him.

"You'll find out. Should be here any minute."

"Why are you doing this?" She persisted.

He turned at the noise of the door opening in the other room.

"I'll let the boss man explain it himself," her captor sneered.

Hayley maintained her position, hoped neither of the men would see she had freed herself until it was too late.

Once again, she experienced a fluttering in her stomach and tightening in her chest as she awaited her first glimpse of the goon who had placed the bounty on her head. Sent an army of assassins after her.

The first man shifted, leaned against the dresser when the newcomer sauntered inside. He was average height, muscular like he worked out but didn't possess the strength of the other man. His face was oblong, with a pointed chin, high cheeks, long nose and thin lips; his groomed midnight black hair was combed back from a wide forehead.

Hayley saw past the disguise of the beard and moustache, recognized Simon Ortiz's piercing black eyes from the picture in the newspaper.

He was dressed in a dark business suit and crisp white shirt, as if he'd just stepped from a corporate board meeting or enterprising fundraiser. Hayley could imagine people mistaking him for a business tycoon with his delicate hands, long manicured fingers that looked like they were used to shuffling papers, giving orders, not manual labor.

She could also understand how Katherine Jenkins would be awed by his charm.

Hayley scowled at the man, refused to let Simon Ortiz intimidate her. She recalled all the anger she'd channeled toward his father for killing Judith and ending her modeling career, added to it the fury for the son who had traumatized her more, killed Savannah and contracted an army of assassins to kill her.

Reminded herself she had survived once, and she would do it again. She would somehow overcome this evil and find Liam.

Simon Ortiz gave Hayley a sly smile. “A sight for sore eyes. Been a long five years but I finally have you where I want you.”

Determined not to let him intimidate her, Hayley pressed her lips together, raised her chin and maintained strong eye contact. Kept her voice firm. “I don’t understand your urgency to kill me. Your father killed my friend. He’s the one in prison, I had nothing to do with you.”

“Oh, but you did. You came back from the dead and in one little blow, destroyed all I’d started to build. All I’d put in place.”

Hayley blinked. “I had nothing to do with you. I testified what happened to me, turned over the evidence that convicted your father.”

“And took away my inheritance. The funds I’d counted on to expand my European ventures. You see, my old man had discovered I was skimming some of his profits, but he thought Judith was setting it up, not me. I decided not to tell him otherwise.”

He pulled a pack of cigarettes from his jacket pocket, lit one, blew the smoke toward the ceiling.

“It was going as planned until Judith started catching the discrepancies. Got suspicious, started talking to Sebastian, gathering her evidence. Saying my old man was crooked. I decided I needed to dispose of her. I’d already faked my death, begun transferring funds. So, I slipped back, took her out of the picture and everything was back to normal until you made your surprise appearance, and everything was frozen.”

Shoulders pushed back against the mattress, Hayley listened, focused on Ortiz while her mind ran through what she needed to do. Keep him talking, give Liam time to locate her, rest her body enough to fight if she had to.

"So, you framed your father?"

"Why not? He was already losing his marbles anyway. Why not let the state take care of him inside a jail cell instead of me. Almost succeeded until you showed up in court."

"Judith did the backups; I simply passed the information along. You killed my friend."

"She took away my inheritance," he shouted, threw the cigarette aside, charged across the room to lean over her. "I had plans for that money. Sat in the courtroom, watched the trial. Things were going well until you showed up and dropped your little bombshell."

"How did you find me?"

"Wasn't easy, believe me." He brushed his hands through his hair, tucked his hands in his pockets when he turned to walk back to the door. "I kept seeing the Hughes bitch at all your father's fundraisers. Did a little research and discovered she was a friend of yours. Found out she was buddy-buddy with this big-time author nobody ever met and put two and two together. Started schmoozing her but she didn't want to talk too much. So, I let my friend here have a go with her and the rest they say is history."

"Why be so vindictive? So greedy?"

"You want to talk about greed, bitch? Your father has always been the greedy one. Always sabotaging anything my family has attempted."

"My father does so much good," Hayley raised her chin, lifted her chest and shoulders as she defended her father in anger. "He has helped so many people. What did he ever do to you and your family?"

"Stood in the way of my own father's attempts for quick cash. Interfered with real estate deals. This house and property for one. Didn't affect my father at the time, the stupid realtor caught the bad rap, but it put some suspicion on us. We had plans for this property. Out of the way, in the country, we'd use the barn for bagging the drugs, house for stashing the girls till we could move them. I managed to snag it when your father decided his subdivision plan wasn't worth the effort. But we got our justice. That accident that killed your mother?"

Hayley stiffened, narrowed her eyes on him. "She lost control of her car."

Simon Ortiz sneered. "Ever wonder what caused her to lose control?"

It was all Hayley could do to restrain the rage that overwhelmed her, resist the sudden urge to jump up and attack the monster that had the gall to brag about playing a part in her mother's death.

"And that car bombing that killed your father's assistant? Her little girl? My father ranted for days because your old man escaped that and wasn't dead."

Hayley gasped to think that this despicable man was also responsible for Grace and Zoe's deaths. And the driver. She jumped when she was certain she identified Liam's voice from the side of the bed.

Simon Ortiz heard it as well and looked down to spot her cellphone on the floor. He grabbed it, threw it across the room.

"You didn't frisk her?" Simon Ortiz's face reddened in anger when he turned on the other man who'd been enjoying the show.

"She was out cold," he defended himself.

"Can any of you idiots do anything right?" Ortiz shouted in anger.

"I got her, didn't I?" The guy raised a hand in defense. "Made a clean getaway."

Hayley's eyes grew round when she witnessed Ortiz pull a pistol from behind his back and aimed it at the guy's stomach. Shot before the man realized he'd been targeted. He lunged for Ortiz but quickly dropped to the floor at the second shot to the head.

Hayley realized she needed to act fast, or she would be next. Her muscles tightened in readiness; she rolled off the bed away from Ortiz. Grabbed the lamp on the night table and tossed it at Ortiz just as he turned back to her. The surprise of the attack and jolt of the lamp against his shoulder threw him off balance but not before he fired another shot into the wall, missed her by inches.

Her adrenaline in overdrive, Hayley began tossing pillows at him while she leaped onto the bed and off, managed to give Ortiz a solid kick in the chest before she landed on her feet. Ortiz fell backwards through the door into the front room.

She sprinted past him, but Ortiz grabbed her ankle, caused her to fall to her knees. She fought the pain that coursed through her body when she rolled on her side, delivered a palm heel strike to his chin, brought her knee up to his crotch.

Ortiz yelled out at the pain, grabbed for her neck to choke her but Hayley managed to give him another elbow strike to his nose. He fell back and Hayley scrambled up, ran out of the door into the darkness.

Chapter Twenty-Two

"It's Hayley," Liam was shocked to recognize Hayley's number on his phone, more so when he overheard her firm voice before he answered. He stopped in his tracks, concentrated on her dialog with the male response.

"She's in trouble," he whispered. "Let's go."

Screaming muscles, a throbbing head and arm, dizziness from the sudden movement prevented Liam from sprinting to Brandon's truck. Once again, Brandon had to help him onto the seat. Liam put the phone on speaker then switched to the app that was still tracking Hayley's location.

Brandon synced his phone to Liam's, studied the GPS location that flashed onto the screen of the truck's dashboard. Calculated their ETA to be twenty minutes. He headed for the interstate, raced in the direction of the tiny blinking dot. Hoped Hayley could maintain her fierce, strong demeanor with her captor.

They listened to Hayley's conversation with Simon Ortiz, shook their heads in amazement at the way he bragged about swindling his father, faking his death, letting his father take the blame for Judith's murder.

"There," Liam whispered, motioned the exit up ahead.

Brandon eased off the interstate, turned onto a dark two-lane road. Slowed to navigate the curves while keeping an eye on the screen for their next turn. He calculated they were five minutes away.

Both men continued to listen and exchanged shocked expressions when Ortiz talked about sabotaging Julia Turner's car. Brandon had suspected foul play but never guessed Simon Ortiz to be the culprit.

When Liam couldn't restrain his reaction to the boast about Grace and Zoe's murders, Brandon worried Ortiz might have picked up on his voice because there were raised male voices of an immediate argument, gunshots, then silence.

Brandon grabbed his phone and dialed nine-one-one, relayed the vicinity of a hostage situation to the dispatcher. They didn't know what had happened, hoped Hayley hadn't got caught in the crossfire.

They almost missed the turn.

"There," Liam yelled when he glimpsed the opening in the woods on their left, held on when Brandon swerved sharply. As much as they wanted to hurry, they didn't want to spook Ortiz.

They followed the narrow drive for a hundred yards before it opened to long bare fields on both sides of the path. The moon was in its last quarter and offered enough light to make out shapes. Brandon dimmed the lights when they spied a grove of trees up ahead, security light on a barn off to the right.

As they approached the grove of trees, they spotted the interior lights of the house. Brandon cut the engine, let the truck coast to a stop beside two vehicles parked in front of what appeared to be an abandoned house. The front door was wide open, and it was quiet.

Both men leaped from the truck. Their handguns drawn, they charged inside, moved like cats stalking a mouse as they scoped the front room, peeked around corners, searched the other areas.

They discovered the man dead on the floor of the bedroom, bullet hole in the wall. Thankful there was no other visible blood.

It concerned Liam there was no sign of Hayley. He checked his phone.

"It's still blinking. She's got to be here somewhere."

Liam searched under the bed, inside the closet but found no one else in the room. He returned to the front room, glanced over to spot Hayley's necklace on the floor.

"They can't be far," Brandon assured his friend.

Liam grabbed the necklace, allowed Murdock to sniff it.

"Go find her," he commanded the dog.

His nose to the floor, Murdock raced out into the darkness.

Hayley hid in the darkness. Rubbed her throat where Ortiz had tried to choke her. Her eyes went round when she realized the necklace wasn't there. Tears glistened when she experienced a momentary scare. What would she do? Her armor, security blanket was gone.

You will take this monster down, she encouraged herself. You got away from him, didn't you? She recalled fighting with Ortiz, wounding him before running out the door into the darkness.

She'd stumbled away from the house, realized she was in the middle of nowhere and had no idea what surrounded her. She gave her eyes a minute to adjust, looked left to right, turned in a circle. Detected the cars from the light of the house reflecting off the hoods.

The Moon's murky rays cast a pale light across open fields the other side of the trees. She made out a border of trees in the distance but was certain she couldn't escape to the woods without Ortiz observing her racing across the open fields.

She'd jumped when she overheard Ortiz yell as he stumbled over a chair in the house behind her. Realized he would be coming after her any second. She spied what appeared to be a barn a hundred yards from the house. Stuck to the shadows as she rushed to the structure, thankful there was no lock on the doors. She'd lifted the latch, heard the groan of the wood as she nudged the door open and slipped inside.

Now she stood in the darkness. Without her necklace. Realized she needed to hide before Ortiz found her. She put her hand out as she made her way across the open area, bumped into something big and cold. Brushed her fingers against what seemed to be rubber, spanned the area, decided it was a humongous tire as the top was two feet above her head.

She edged her way past the rounded tire, banged her knee against the hard metal of a hitch, sought the second tire. Now she was familiar with the lay of her corner, she decided she'd stay close to the door for a fast escape if he should search the other side of the barn.

Hayley paused when she caught the groaning of the door a second time, jumped when the door banged against the building. He'd left the door open, but it was still dark when she peeked around the tire, followed his movements as he shined a flashlight into the dark corners. She was thankful she was behind the big tire when it scoped the tractor.

She inched her way along the side of the tractor around to the front while he progressed in the opposite direction. Intended to escape via the door while he searched the center of the big room.

Hayley squeezed her eyes shut in frustration when her shoe bumped into what must have been an aluminum bucket. She froze when the noise sounded like a shot in the dark in the quiet still barn.

Ortiz turned quickly, moved toward the tractor. Pinned her in place when the bright glare of the flashlight blinded her.

Murdock raced toward the barn, his nose tracking the fresh scent of his mistress. He charged through the door, alerted to the unfamiliar human, picked up on the tension emanating from him. Caught a whiff of the fresh gunpowder and jumped into attack mode locking his jaws onto the arm that aimed the gun.

Hayley cried out, thankful Murdock had come to her rescue. That meant Lian was nearby.

She worried Ortiz might shoot Murdock, knew she needed to do something; couldn't sit and wait for Liam to arrive. She stumbled over a wooden tool, reached down to grab it, realized it was a long-handled tool. Recognized it to be a rake. An antique rake with wide, metal claws.

She gripped her hands around the metal part, raced out toward the beam of light that was bobbing because of Murdock's mighty grip on Ortiz's arm. She started swinging high and managed to connect with the man's back with a solid whack.

Ortiz hollered out loud, dropped the flashlight when he fell to the floor.

Hayley raced over for the flashlight; thankful it was a heavy-duty case. She located her quarry and began beating the semi-conscious Ortiz over the head with the rounded lamp.

Five years of pent-up anger surged through her body.

"This is for my mother." She struck him hard.

"This one's for Judith," she struck again. "And Savannah. Grace and Zoe," she hit him again and again, one for each of her loved ones he had killed.

Murdock jumped in place, barking his encouragement.

Suddenly the interior of the barn was bright with the headlights of Brandon's truck. Liam hastened across the room, grabbed for the bloody flashlight before Hayley could bludgeon the unconscious man.

He tossed the flashlight aside, ignored the pain shooting through his injured arm as he wrapped his arms around Hayley, tried to console her.

"Red," he spoke into her ear, "It's okay. He's down. Hayley, you're okay."

Hayley was breathing hard; her body shook with adrenaline. She fought against the arms that tightened around her until Liam's voice registered in her ear. Then she collapsed and the fear, anger, melted away, replaced by wails and sobs a deep sense of relief that it was behind her. Sorrow to know her mother had been murdered.

She wrapped her arms around his middle and hung on, thankful he was okay, trying to comfort her.

Hayley, Brandon and Liam leaned against the truck, waited while the paramedics loaded an unconscious Simon Ortiz into the ambulance, his partner into the hearse.

They had given their statements and were released to go but Hayley refused to leave until she was certain Ortiz was in police custody. She called out to the state trooper overseeing the transfer.

"Make sure he's handcuffed to that gurney. I don't want him to miss his court date."

Liam and Brandon chuckled; the trooper shook his head and waved.

Hayley's mouth curved into a smile as they loaded into Brandon's truck and followed the vehicles away from the abandoned house with yellow police tape across the windows and front door.

An hour later, Hayley stepped out of the shower of their hotel room refreshed and alive. She'd scrubbed her body, lathered her hair with vigor multiple times, determined to remove any trace of Simon Ortiz from her person.

She found Liam dozing on the bed. Considering his condition, she'd let him have first dibs in the shower, figured he would be fast asleep by the time she finished hers.

Her eyes travelled over the bruises covering the left side of his body from his shoulder past his hip. Her eyes filled with tears when they rested on the bandaged arm, imagined how their evening could have ended so differently.

She jumped when his eyes opened, and he stared into hers.

"I was so scared you'd been killed," she whispered. Rubbed her hands up and down her arms when an intense shiver thrilled through her body.

"I'm curious though, how did you find me? My phone?"

Liam shook his head, nodded to his jeans on the other bed. "Check my pockets."

Hayley's eyes brightened when she discovered her necklace tucked inside.

"My necklace, I thought I'd lost it." She frowned as she sat on the bed beside him. "Wait. You're saying you found me because of my necklace?"

Liam turned the design over, pointed to the back of the single diamond mounted in the center of the Celtic knot.

"It's hard to detect but I had a tracker embedded behind the diamond."

"You. You gave me the necklace? But you let me think my father gave it to me."

"It's a Celtic love knot. See how the knots interlace to form the heart? One heart is facing downward, the other upward. This necklace was the only way I could give you the independence you craved. Much as I didn't want to let you go, I needed some assurance you would be okay. I knew you wouldn't accept it from me, so I left it for you to find."

Hayley's breath hitched as warmth spread through her. It amazed her that he had loved her for so long. Had let her go so she could be happy.

"Good thing I took a liking to it and wore it all the time."

Liam pursed his lips. "That was a concern at first, but I figured you wouldn't resist wearing something so sparkling."

"So," she hooked the necklace around her neck, stood to remove her bathrobe, tossed it onto the bed beside his jeans, "you think I'm invincible?"

The corners of his lips curved into a smile. "Red, after tonight, I'm convinced you are indestructible." He swallowed when she straddled him. Brushed her damp hair away from her shoulders.

"You know," she brushed her hands across his bare chest, "now that Ortiz is out of my life, and I've proven I'm indestructible, I won't need you to protect me."

"That anxious to get rid of me?" Liam spoke out of the corner of his mouth, his eyes turning dark.

Hayley laughed out loud. "Oh no, I have other plans." She leaned down to brush her breasts across his chest while she nibbled his chin. "I'll play nurse for a while, get you recovered." She kissed a cheek. "You're my inspiration," she kissed his other cheek then his forehead. "I have lots more plots and what ifs to pursue with you to stimulate me," she whispered in his ear before her mouth took hungry possession of his.

Epilog

"Nervous?" Liam asked as he hooked the necklace around Hayley's neck. Brushed his lips along the side of her neck.

"Yes, and no." Hayley gushed, shivered at the endearment.

It had been six months since that volatile night when Simon Ortiz met his match. He suffered through a painful recovery, sat through a week-long trial, sneered when he'd been convicted and sentenced to life in prison. Would have joined his father in the same prison if William Ortiz hadn't succumbed to the Alzheimer's days before his son's trial began.

During the investigation of Simon Ortiz's many crimes, it was discovered he had also orchestrated the murder of Katherine Jenkins' husband.

Hayley and Liam witnessed every day of the trial, celebrated with her father when the conviction was handed down.

Hayley observed the detectives and special consultants called in to testify. Took copious notes and used many of the observations to finish Faith and Kyle's story. The book was released earlier that day, and, in an hour, Hayley would be divulging the identity of Jillian

McLeod to the world at a cocktail party sponsored by her father.

The nightmares had stopped, and Liam remained by her side worked to expand his security business while Hayley continued her writing.

Liam turned her, studied the necklace, appreciated the long luscious auburn hair arranged in loose curls atop her head, two stray strands on either side of her face. She was dressed in a classic navy blue dress with an embroidered bodice and off-shoulder straps spattered with white sparkles. The empire A-line chiffon skirt was short in front to highlight her slender legs, cascaded to the floor in back. He decided she'd never look more beautiful.

"Before we leave, I wanted to give you something to compliment the necklace."

"A prize for finishing the book?"

"Not exactly," he smiled as he opened the square black box.

Hayley's eyes grew wide when she stared at a miniature of the necklace designed into the ring. The smaller interlacing knots were a snug fit around the two-carat diamond.

"Took the jeweler some time to put this together. If you like it, there's a matching band we can add when we get married next month."

"Next month, huh?" This was the first she'd heard of marriage. She let him slip the ring on her finger, held her hand up to admire it when she wrapped her arms around his neck. "Why wait that long?" Her mouth curved into a smile as she offered her lips to his.

ABOUT KAY

As a teenager, Kay enjoyed reading Georgette Heyer, Daphne duMaurier, Mary Stewart and Victoria Holt and treasured the ones she collected.

She discovered contemporary romance when she needed something light to read while her children were napping, found herself wondering "what if" and decided to write a story of her own.

Three small children, a full-time job as a Library Director, Little League and civic obligations required that she put the pen away for a while, although she continued to write news articles and library newsletters. She became immersed in the community and made friends with many of the citizens through the library.

In 2007, she and her husband opened a wine shop – Grapes of Taste – and the people she didn't know through the library became friends at their wine tastings in the shop.

In 2013, Kay retired from the library, began reading again, pulled out her old manuscripts. Once again, she found herself wondering, what if I make a change here? A change there? Update things?

She closed the wine shop in 2015 and has been seriously writing ever since.

There are many more "what if" stories waiting to come alive.

Please enjoy her website, www.kaydbrooksauthor.com
Facebook page: Kay Brooks (author)
She also welcomes comments via email:
kaydbrooks.author@gmail.com

Made in the USA
Middletown, DE
19 June 2023